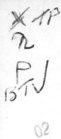

X 1P
2
P
BTV

02

D0993828

ROGUE COLT

He was a gunfighter if ever they had seen one — there was no mistaking that custom-built Peacemaker. But for the farming folk fighting for survival, there was more than the fate of a half-dead stranger to reckon on. They faced the evil-minded Larsen, cold-bloodedly 'persuading' them to quit the territory and move on. There seemed no respite from his brutal tactics — until the wounded stranger disappeared, and the Peacemaker began to blaze . . .

LUTHER CHANCE

ROGUE COLT

Complete and Unabridged

LINFORD
Leicester

First published in Great Britain in 2000 by
Robert Hale Limited
London

First Linford Edition
published 2001
by arrangement with
Robert Hale Limited
London

British Library CIP Data

Chance, Luther
  Rogue colt.—Large print ed.—
Linford western library
  1. Western stories
  2. Large type books
  I. Title
  823.9'14 [F]

  ISBN 0–7089–4559–7

Published by
F. A. Thorpe (Publishing)
Anstey, Leicestershire

Set by Words & Graphics Ltd.
Anstey, Leicestershire
Printed and bound in Great Britain by
T. J. International Ltd., Padstow, Cornwall

This book is printed on acid-free paper

This for K
when the horizons beckon

1

He would be dead before noon, maybe sooner now that the trail had scattered, the land emptied to a scorched inferno and even the rattlers taken to shade.

Dead as bad meat, but not buried decent and no marker to show it. Nothing, come the whip of hot winds and days of high sun, save the rags of torn clothes, a broad-brimmed black hat, belt, boots and bleached white bones.

And the Colt.

Whoever it was happened that way would spot the weathered sheen of the gun, sure enough, lift it from the sand, feel the smooth, easy shape to the butt, note the long fitted barrel, Peacemaker style, spin the chamber, twice to be certain, and figure for a fact that the shell of the fellow sandswept at their feet had once housed a gunslinger down on his luck.

Way down, they might reckon, seeing as how he had trailed five miles into the Badlands; probably wounded, bleeding fast, out of water and heat-soaked to exhaustion. Would have made it this far, to the rock-strewn drift to the creek, slid from his mount and crawled the short distance to the twist of thin shade at the straggle of brush. Only a matter of time then before the horse strayed and the fellow breathed his last.

Well, maybe he had got what was coming, just like most of his kind always did: another town, another swaggering, Colt-crazed kid to be outgunned, only this time a fraction faster, sharper, catching the fellow off his guard and a mite too relaxed. Call it rough justice, but that was the way of things. Live by the gun, and you sure as hell came to die by it.

Even so, this fellow would have hung on to the last, whoever he was. But out here, in this heat, with the nearest water a day's ride north, he would have been no better than the next. Just a man when all was said and finally done.

Handsome-looking Colt, though . . .

*   *   *

Esme Green dried her hands carefully on the cloth, taking time for a moment to burnish the gleam of her wedding ring, patted the stray wisps of hair into place at her neck, smoothed the folds of her skirt and went almost on tiptoe to the door at the shadowed end of the homestead's living-room.

No good reason she could think to, of course, why she should be so quiet, just that it seemed natural, almost polite, not to disturb a sleeping body without fair warning. Especially the body back of the door there. No saying how the fellow might react once he opened his eyes and realized he was still alive.

If he ever did.

She leaned closer to the door and listened for the slightest change of note to the dull, rhythmic lift and fall of the breathing. Same as ever, she thought, with a gentle sigh. Same as it had been these past four days, ever since her husband, Clyde, Joe Medley and Henry Keyes had brought the fellow in more dead than alive from the Utepan.

Some mess too, she recalled, her gaze soft and unblinking on the window and the fading glow of dusk beyond it. Been about this time of day when the three of them had carried the sun-scorched, blood-smeared body indoors and stood a while simply staring at it, uncertain then of whether to set to bathing it or dig a hole and bury it.

Odds had been on the shovels until she had come to kneel at the man's side and notice the merest flicker of movement in his fingers . . .

'Water, hot and cold, cloths and bandagin', quick as yuh can,' she had ordered and begun the grisly job of easing the rags that had once been clothes from the near charred body.

'Bad shape, ain't he?' Joe had said, squatting to help her. 'Clyde spotted a

4

stray mount, fine-lookin' mare, quarter-mile or so into the 'Pan. Rounded it up, but reckoned we should go take a look, mebbe find the rider. Hell, we trailed best part of the day, gettin' deeper. All for throwin' it in when we eyed the buzzards, six of 'em, circlin' like death up there. Never figured for findin' a body still breathin'.' Joe had gulped and winced then at the sight of the exposed wound deep in the man's chest. 'Sufferin' dogs, Esme, that's gunshot, no mistake. Miracle he ain't long dead.'

'Not yet it ain't,' was all she had found voice enough to murmur.

It had taken a painful, anxious two hours to clean the man to a recognizable shape, a body with arms and legs and a face behind the mask of dust, dirt and sunburn, wash the clotted blood from the wound, treat it best they knew how from the few medicines they could summon, bandage it and lift the fellow from the living-room floor to the bed in the homestead's spare room.

The miracle then, to Esme Green's

reckoning, was that he, was still breathing, albeit faint and sometimes weakening, but sufficient to cling to some frail thread of life. For how long, and through what depths of agony, only Fate and his Maker would decide.

'Needs a doc, don't he?' Henry had said, buttoning the cuffs of his shirt. 'Wound like that . . . Hell, wouldn't surprise me none if there ain't lead still buried there.'

'You volunteerin' to go fetch him?' Joe had clipped, raising a careful eyebrow. 'Yuh got the stomach for ridin' into town?'

'Hell, no, 'course I ain't. Have you?'

'Know better than to set foot there, don't I?' Henry had mumbled, his glance shifting quickly from Esme to her husband.

'Same as we all do. But don't ask me how much longer we're goin' to hold out — '

'Let's not get into that again,' Clyde had said, turning from the bed. 'Not now. T'ain't the time. We got to look

6

to the fella here.'

Henry had folded his arms dramatically. 'So it's like I'm sayin', ain't it? Fella needs a doc. Won't last the night if he don't. Damnit, just about anybody can see that. And where's the doc? Why, right there in Mission, three miles down the trail. Simple — 'ceptin' there ain't a homesteader among us who'd risk his neck within a sight of town. Not while Larsen's runnin' it, he wouldn't. We all seen what happens when yuh do. Sep Kline risked it, darn fool, and we brought him back. Sure we did — stiff as a board back of my wagon!'

'Hold on there, Henry,' Clyde had gestured. 'Yuh gettin' this outa proportion. We're talkin' about a dyin' fella here.'

'Yuh figure that for makin' a difference?'

'Sure I do. Doc'd see it that way.'

'*He* might,' Joe had scoffed, 'but Larsen sure as hell wouldn't. Like as not put the fella out of his misery and one of us to keep him company! All of

7

us if he had a mind to.'

'That's the size of it, Clyde,' Henry had added, loosening his arms to his sides. 'Can't say other, can yuh? And it ain't goin' to change one spit, not so long as we're sittin' where we are on land that railroad company back East wants at any price. *Any price* — even killin' for.'

'I know, I know,' Clyde had sighed impatiently. 'We all know, but Larsen ain't the company, only their hired man here, and if they got to hearin' how he's handlin' things — '

'Hell, Clyde, can't yuh ever get it into yuh head we ain't wanted here? We're trash litterin' the land, holdin' things up, costin' them Eastern fancy-pants a whole heap of hard cash and time. They ain't fussed none how Larsen shifts us, only that he does. Who are we, f'Cris'sake? No more than homestea-din', sodbustin' scum, dust to be blown away, thrown out.' Henry had folded his arms again, fixed his lips to a tight line, and narrowed his tired grey eyes to

8

ghostly slits. 'Sep Kline last week . . . So who's next, Clyde? Joe here, m'self, you? Yuh goin' to leave Esme a widow before she's had half a chance to be a wife?'

'That's fool talk, Henry Keyes,' Clyde had flared, but been halted in his outburst by Esme's despairing groan and swirl of the shawl at her shoulders.

'Will yuh just stop it, all of yuh? How many times yuh all said this? How many nights yuh spent rantin' round it, debatin' it, arguin'? Weeks, months? Hell, don't we all wake wonderin' if this'll be the last day? Don't we all spend best part of it watchin' that trail out there for a sight of Larsen and his sidekicks ridin' in? Ain't we all livin' on figurin' for the next breath bein' the last? Well, ain't we? Let me tell yuh somethin', this fella here sure as hell is, and if we don't get to doin' somethin' about it, and real soon, yuh goin' to see and hear it right there on that bed!'

There had been a moment then of silence, of gazes turned back to the near lifeless body, its burned, blackened face without expression in the blistered twists of skin, the eyes closed, mouth and lips no more than a scrawled crack; a half-dead thing that might have crawled from the bloody fields of carnage.

Esme had shivered and pulled the shawl across her breasts and into her neck — but against the chill of the gathering night, the hopelessness of the body on the bed, the fear of the town, the cold resolve of survival in the harsh homesteading life? She had not been certain; only that the silence and the looks on the faces of the men around her had seemed to be asking the same question.

'Mebbe we did wrong,' Joe had finally murmured, the sound of his voice like the whisper of mist. 'Mebbe we should've finished it out there on the 'Pan. Shot the poor devil where we found him.'

'Somebody tried,' Henry had said without lifting his gaze from the body.

'Mebbe the fella had a price on his head. Might still have, if he lives.'

'Yuh tellin' me we got some sorta gunfighter here?' Esme had frowned. 'That what yuh brought in?'

'Best show her that Colt we found along of him, Clyde,' Joe had grunted. 'Piece like he was carryin' tells yuh all yuh need to know . . .'

★   ★   ★

But that had been four days ago, thought Esme, turning her back to the door, leaning on it, closing her eyes. Four days of watching and nursing the man on the bed, of waiting for death to reach for him, hearing it in the rasp of his breath, the deep moans as the bandaging was changed, the wound cleaned. Wondering if soon there might be the flicker of an eye, some sound . . .

Her eyes opened instantly, wide and staring, at the pound of hoofbeats, swinging, dancing jig of tack, crack of leather. Riders, coming in fast, from the

11

west, the trail out of town.

'Yuh in there, Green?' spat the voice like something chiselled from the sweep of night. 'Get yuh out here, if yuh know what's good for yuh. Now, damn yuh!'

2

Four men, dust-smudged, shabby, unwashed, leaning easy and relaxed to the necks of their sweating mounts, their gazes following Esme's careful steps to the homestead veranda and settling on her like hawks watching a tasty prey.

'Yuh man about, lady?' drawled the leaner, sour-faced leader of the pack as his horse tossed its head against the loosened reins.

'Who's askin'?' said Esme, fingering her shawl, eyes narrowing to sharp, watchful slits across the staring faces, a part of her concentration straying to the darkened window of the room at the back of her and the body on the bed.

'Yuh know well enough. Seen us before, ain't yuh? Got a message from Larsen.'

'My husband's helpin' out with new

fencin' over Charlie Bishop's spread. Won't be here 'til dark.'

The man sniggered. 'Wastin' his time, lady. Ain't no call for new fencin'. Rootin' it out more like! What yuh say, boys?' The men grunted and grinned. 'Larsen wants yuh to know — all of yuh — yuh got three weeks. Yuh hear, three weeks to be off this land and gone? Last time of tellin' yuh.'

'I see,' said Esme, folding her arms as she eased her weight to one hip. 'And if we refuse?'

'Refusin' ain't in it. Yuh go. Simple. Guaranteed safe passage far as the Utepan. On yuh own from there. That plain enough, lady?' The man scratched a slow finger through his stubble. 'Don't have to spell out how it'll be if yuh don't, do I? Yuh know Larsen well enough. He ain't for messin' with.'

'Sure, I know him,' sneered Esme. 'Know him same as I know vermin when I smell it!'

The man stiffened, but shrugged and slid his wet lips to a grin. 'Wouldn't let

14

Larsen hear yuh talkin' like that. Might try his patience some. And yuh sure as hell done plenty of that these past months. Could be he's gotten a mite weary of it, and when Larsen gets weary — well, now, there ain't no reckonin' to him, not for man or woman. 'Specially a woman. I make m'self clear?'

'Don't fret me none, mister,' snapped Esme, already conscious of the trickle of sweat from her brow. 'Yuh can tell him as much — my compliments!'

The man shrugged again. 'I'll do just that, lady. Be a pleasure. Wouldn't wanna be standin' in your boots, though, if it catches him on a bad day. That I surely wouldn't! Meantime . . .' He leaned forward, the grin shading on the gleam of his eyes through the evening gloom as they shifted beyond her for a moment to the shape of the homestead. 'Three weeks, to the day. Make sure yuh man and the rest of them sodbusters hear it loud and clear.'

Esme gripped the shawl and tugged it

15

hard across her shoulders. 'Do yuh worst!' she snapped on a spitting hiss.

The man had half-turned his mount from the veranda, when he paused, waited a moment and swung round in the saddle. 'Yuh seen anythin' of a stranger passin' through these past days?' he asked quietly.

'Don't nobody pass through here savin' if they're lost,' quipped Esme, suddenly tense and stiff. 'T'ain't healthy!'

'Mebbe, but you just let Larsen know if yuh do, eh? Might earn yuh a reprieve!'

'Oh, sure,' mocked Esme, 'I'll do just that, minute I set eyes on the fella! So who am I lookin' for? Another piece of farm-bustin' scum? Wouldn't take a deal of spottin' seein' as how I seen so many of 'em!'

'Yuh got some whippy tongue there, lady, and no mistake, and if I had the way of it right now I'd beat them sassy words clean outa yuh. Reckon y'self lucky me and the boys ain't got the

16

time. You just keep an eye for the stranger. Tall fella, rides a dark mare. No mistakin' him for bein' what he is.'

'Oh,' said Esme, a shiver twitching across her shoulders, 'and what might that be?'

'Size of the Colt he holsters stakes him for a gunfighter. Wild with it, so don't tangle, not if yuh wanna see the Utepan. Leave him to Larsen. It's personal.'

'He got a name?' called Esme, as the riders cleared the spread and headed into the gloom.

'Don't use one,' yelled the sour-faced man. 'Got no need. Colt marks him out.'

Esme was still shivering when the land lay silent again under the closing night and she turned to stare at the darkened window, a deep frown furrowing her sweating brow.

★ ★ ★

'Hell, will somebody tell me I'm dreamin' this, that it ain't for real? T'ain't is it?' Joe Medley stalked from the flickering glow of lantern light to the hanging shadows at the end of the barn, grunted to himself, then turned quickly to the men grouped round the flame. 'Well?' was all he croaked, slipping his hands to his trousers pockets.

'Real enough, Joe,' sighed Charlie Bishop, wiping his grey-dusted stubble. 'Esme ain't one for exaggeratin'. What she says is what we got.'

'And that's just one helluva heap of trouble,' groaned Frank Cooper, leaning back from the light to a straw bale. 'Strikes me Larsen ain't foolin' none in that threat. Three weeks . . . and then what? His boys goin' to just ride in, shoot us where we stand if we ain't all packed and set to move on? That simple? Damn it, t'ain't human.'

'Who's talkin' 'human'? Larsen sure ain't human. Hatched him back of Hell, didn't they?'

'But that ain't the half of it, is it?' murmured Henry Keyes, staring into the palms of his worn, calloused hands. 'There's the man, ain't there? The gunfighter, if that's who he is. What we goin' to do about him? Yuh heard what Esme said. If Larsen's lookin' for the fella, how long's it going to be before he finds him, right here, under Clyde's roof, bein' nursed by Clyde's wife? Hell, what then? I'll tell yuh what then — '

'Save it,' said Clyde Green, his gaze springing like a surge of the flame to Keyes' face. 'Talk like that don't serve no purpose.'

'So what yuh goin' to do, Clyde?' asked Joe from the shadows. 'Yuh goin' to sit it out same as yuh've always said? Gettin' a mite too heated for my likin'.'

'We've held out this far, and rightly so. Land we got here is claimed legal, papers with them agents and attorneys back East. Ain't nobody walkin' this earth can just take it, not even some high-struttin' railroad company. And money can't buy it, 'ceptin' on our say-so. But there's other ways, ain't there — like gettin' a scumbag style of Larsen to do the dirty work for yuh? Ain't no amount of paperwork goin' to stop him, not when there ain't a stitch of law this side of the 'Pan that ain't sittin' in Larsen's pocket or too feared to move against him.'

'Yuh right, Joe,' said Frank, leaning forward from the bale to the spread of light. 'Paperwork don't stand to protectin' wives and young 'uns. Paper ain't guns and before yuh say it, there ain't one of us here with a spit of a chance in some gunslingin' showdown with Larsen.' He stared at his boots. 'Been five, dirt-grindin' years gettin' my place to some sorta shape, but, hell, wife and a clutch of kids gotta come first. Ain't no choice.'

'Yuh'd pull out?' croaked Henry.

Frank raised a flat, wet gaze to the glow. 'Get started sun-up,' he whispered.

'Now, wait. Just hold it,' said Clyde

through a sudden stride from the lantern. 'We gotta talk this out proper.'

'We been *talkin'* for twelve whole months,' snapped Charlie.

'T'ain't got us nowhere,' said Joe.

'All we got from talkin' is Sep Kline pushin' up plains' weed,' added Frank.

'I know. I hear yuh every word, and believe me they hurt, same as they do for all of yuh, but if we back down now, give Larsen half an edge . . . ' Clyde thudded a fist to the flesh of a hand. 'We do that, and we're finished. Land, homes, families, not worth the dirt on yuh boots. And don't go thinkin' yuh can start up again some place else. Yuh won't, 'cus there'll be another Larsen waitin' on yuh, movin' yuh on, gunnin' yuh out 'til there ain't no places left and yuh end yuh days somewhere dead as the Utepan and a self-respect to match.' The man's eyes flashed as he swallowed, long and deep, and the race of his heart pounded at his chest. 'That what yuh plannin' on? That what yuh been scratchin' and diggin' and ploughin' this land to inherit? Well, I'll tell yuh somethin', all of yuh — '

His eyes flashed again as he raised them in a wide stare to the creak and grind of the barn door being dragged open.

'Fire, over Charlie's place!' gasped Esme, the sweat gleaming on her face as the night sky behind her filled with the surge of licking flames.

3

It took the five men only minutes to douse the lantern, break from the barn to their mounts, Esme scurrying in their wake, and ride hard, fast, low-slung and in silence from the homestead towards the furnace of blaze.

Grey dust swirled like the breath of night ghosts to the pound of hoofs, shadows leapt on the flame-bruised light, smoke swung wild and shapeless in mountainous palls, and the high moon, wide and round as a startled eye, seemed to stare as if frozen in shock.

Clyde led the dash, his gaze tightened to slits against the rush of hot air and flying cinders, and was the first to see the scattered new fencing, the posts ripped from their roots and tossed to the dirt like old bones, the cross timbers smashed and splintered.

'Goddamnit, look what they done, the bastards!' yelled Charlie, closing on Clyde, his face a mass of lathered sweat and creased, twitching anger.

Bad enough, thought Clyde, through his own surge of anger churning in the pit of his stomach, but as nothing to the flaring flames of the torched barn ahead of them.

'Hell, my barn!' groaned Charlie behind the snorting fear of his mount.

'Larsen gone clean out of his head?' bellowed Henry.

'Mary Jo and the kids — anybody see 'em?' groaned Charlie again.

I see 'em,' called Frank Cooper. 'Right there, far side of the homestead.'

'Leave 'em to me,' shouted Esme, swinging her mount clear of the others. 'Save what yuh can at the barn.'

The men rode on, the horses skidding in a frenzy near to panic but held tight on short reins, the whites of their eyes gleaming against the sudden billows of smoke, flashing at the twisting spirals of sparks.

'Split up, left and right,' ordered Clyde, gesturing with an outstretched arm.

'T'ain't no use, Clyde,' gasped Joe Medley, one hand swishing to clear the smoke in a shower of ash and cinders. 'Place is goin' up.'

'We gotta try, damn it!'

The sound of Clyde's croaked curse seemed to echo behind the pounding hoofs, the crackling hiss and roar of the flaming timbers, and then as instantly be smothered in an explosive thrust and rush of fire from the very heart of the barn as if, in one fast gluttonous gorge on its prey, the flames had swallowed the place whole and vomited on their greed.

The mounts slithered, skewed sideways, rose high on their backlegs and whinnied and snorted to a crashing, foaming halt.

Henry Keyes lost his grip on the reins and grabbed with both arms for his horse's neck; Joe Medley groaned and bellowed and crunched back into his saddle with a sickening butt-bruising thud; Frank Cooper's head threatened to be wrenched from his neck and shoulders like a ball of cottongrass lifted in a wildcat twister, before he was dumped to the dirt in a sprawl of arms and legs; Charlie Bishop yelled at the top of his voice, slipped his hold with hands and knees and was flung from his mount in a swirling heap of flapping shirt-tails and split pants; Clyde Green's mount bucked and veered into a snorting, racing dash for the deepest of the night shadows, throwing its rider face-down across a spiky, ash-laced straggle of grass.

The barn erupted again, shattering the roof to the chewed parings of a giant toothpick in a rush and gush of air that raced for the moon like a hissing belch. And for a moment then there was an almost stifling silence, an eerie stillness, before the fire burned on, licking softly at the already charred and blackened remains.

Somewhere a child's scream faded.

A horse whinnied, another snorted.

A woman sobbed. A timber crashed. Sparks flew like scorched flies.

The moon blinked on a lazy curl of smoke.

Clyde staggered to his feet, blinking on dust and dirt, swallowing then choking as he gazed over the lunging shadows and still flame-lit glow across the land.

'We all here?' he called, shielding his eyes to probe the glare. 'Charlie, Joe . . . '

'Over here,' croaked Henry.

'Here,' groaned Joe.

'With yuh, Clyde,' choked Frank Cooper. 'Barn's done for.'

'Where's Charlie, damn it?' called Clyde again.

The four men gathered, dusty, bedraggled, sweat-stained and breathless, their tight, anxious stares swinging in turn from the blaze to the huddled group of Charlie's family and Esme on the steps to the homestead, to the blaze again and then into the darker depths where it was near impossible to distinguish solid shapes from shadows, moonlight from flame.

'He ain't in there, is he?' croaked Henry, squinting into the burning barn.

'Last I seen he was grovellin' back there in the dirt,' said Frank.

'Darn fool's mebbe gotten himself — '

Joe swung round with the others at the beat of hoofs far to their right, the suddenly looming shapes of a half-dozen riders spurring their mounts from the darkness like phantoms.

'Hell,' moaned Joe, 'them's Larsen's men. They ain't done yet!'

'Sons-of-goddamn-bitches,' murmured Frank as he raised a shaking hand to his lathered face.

'Don't move,' snapped Clyde. 'Let 'em come.'

'We got any choice?' grated Joe, his voice as heavy as stone.

The riders closed, veering first left, then right, swinging to a pounding line, regrouping as they headed for the watching men.

'Don't scatter!' yelled Clyde. 'Hold yuh ground!'

Frank Cooper groaned and shuddered. Joe twitched and settled a hand on his rattling throat. Henry's eyes widened, reflecting the lick of the blaze, the dancing glow, the darkening, swirling shapes of the pounding mounts, and his lips began to move through soundless murmurings.

'I'll see 'em clear into Hell,' hissed Joe through clenched, grinding teeth. 'Or die waitin' on it.'

And well he might have, crushed and kicked to death where he stood, Frank and Henry and Clyde joining him in a scrape of blood and pulp. But not on that night, not there, with his eyes swimming between the torment of destruction and the oncoming rush of terror, and not, as it happened then, in the sight of Charlie Bishop rising from the dirt and scrub to stand firm and square and head-on to the riders.

'Get down, Charlie!' yelled Clyde, lunging forward, only to be checked by a trembling Frank Cooper.

'Down, f'Cris'sake!' yelled Joe, his voice pitching close to a scream.

Charlie's curses rolled from him like thunder. His arms waved and punched high above his head as his whole body shuddered in a spasm of anger and hatred. He fell a step to the path of the pounding hoofs, righted himself to his full height again, shrieked his abuse as the dust began to cloud and circle on the smoke-drenched air like a thickening mist.

Charlie was still standing after the first shot had ripped deep into his chest, still on his feet at the blaze of the second and third. Blood soaked into his shirt and trickled to his waist, his eyes flared, wild and crazed as the sweeping flames, but his legs held and his arms continued to wave until, in one crashing thrust of horse flesh and thudding hoofs, the riders passed over him as if trampling no more than a wayward sprig of brush and swung away to the night.

As the walls of the barn collapsed to charred timber and ash, so Charlie's last groan was drowned in the crash of them.

4

'He's gotta be buried decent. Proper place, proper marker. Poor devil deserves that much. Least we can do.' Joe Medley grunted, sighed and knuckled at the smear of damp on his cheeks. 'As for them scum ... ' He swallowed and turned his tired, red-rimmed stare from the blanket-covered body to the faces of the others gathered in the silence of the breaking first light.

'Don't think on it, Joe,' murmured Clyde, shifting a boot over the ash and dirt. 'Not here, not yet. We got others to look to.'

His gaze narrowed on the smoking remains of the barn, the bones of it scattered across the land like the leftovers of some orgy of feasting, moved on to the homestead where a lone lantern glow lit a window, to the group of women and youngsters hovering uncertainly on the veranda, their faces drained and empty, as ashen as the tentative light and the land it reached, settled for a moment on the slumped, sobbing shape rocking in the creaking chair, Esme among the others bent to the widow's shoulders, then blurred and slid away on a long, wet blink.

'Do the best we can by Mary Jo there and the young 'uns . . . Look to Charlie's affairs, the stock . . . Hell!'

'Sure, we'll do all that, Clyde,' said Henry Keyes, his eyes suddenly sharp and dry, 'but t'ain't all we gotta do, is it? This is murder here. Yuh know that, don't yuh? Ain't no refutin' it.'

'I know,' whispered Clyde.

'All them years, the stinkin' summers, winters froze tight as a sleepin' tick, the work, the dream of it . . . ' droned Henry, staring at the body. 'This what it comes down to — yuh dream and all yuh reap for the back-breakin' sweat of it is a nightmare?

Grave some place and a marker to say yuh died there. That it? Wife and yuh kin left to beggin' for a livin'?'

'Easy there, Henry,' murmured Clyde.

'Easy, f'Cris'sake?' flared Henry. '*Easy*? What the hell's there to be easy over, tell me that? Can't, can yuh? Ain't no sayin' to it. Damnit, what am I supposed to do when I seen what we witnessed here? Go tell Widow Bishop as how she ain't to worry, we'll look to her and them kids cryin' at her skirts, say as how it's all been worth it, Charlie was a good man, good farmer, just gotten unlucky in the aim of some vermin's gun? That what I gotta do? That easy enough for yuh?'

'Yuh known darn well — ' began Clyde.

'End of the line, ain't it?' croaked Frank Cooper. 'Like I said, time to pull out.'

'Yuh can't do that, Frank,' began Clyde again. 'Yuh just can't, yuh hear me?'

'Yuh know what my woman there is

thinkin' right now?' retorted Frank. 'I'll tell yuh: she's thinkin' on how soon we can load our wagons and get the hell out before she's the next waitin' on good neighbours to dig a grave for her man. And yuh know somethin'? Can't say I blame her.'

'Size of it, Clyde,' muttered Joe. 'I'm for decidin' the same. Too much at stake here. Can't risk losin' what little I'm goin' to be left with.'

'And Larsen goes free?' snapped Clyde. 'He walks away, job done, rides out to the next stretch of railroad, next bunch of sodbusters happenin' to be in the wrong place, wrong time? Still, won't be no sweat, will it? No, he'll do like he always does — he'll just kill a few of 'em 'til the rest get the message and up sticks and run! Not no way. Damnit, I'll spill my guts clear across the Utepan sooner than run!'

The others were still standing over the body, still staring, as Clyde Green strode away, about the only thing moving with anything like a purpose through the chilled grey light of that mournful morning.

* * *

Or maybe he was just plain mule-headed, he pondered, an hour later as he made his slow way back to the spread, Esme riding in her own preoccupied silence at his side.

Charlie Bishop had died to no good purpose saving the greed of some land-grabbing railroad company with no thought for the folk whose lives they might end in the quest for the line and the profit it would bring. Life came cheap, death easy, especially when the fellow calling the dirty shots happened to be the likes of Larsen. A hired gun, paid to trouble-shoot and make it fast and permanent. No sweat for Larsen, and no dirty hands for the faceless men back East.

Well, maybe not so easy, he mused, flexing his fingers on the slack rein, not if them financiers got to hear the real

36

story of the cost of the rail; not if somebody could get to them, tell them how it really was, how Larsen operated, the grief, loss and destruction left in his wake. Not if that somebody could spell it out how many bodies for every mile of track . . .

'Want me to read yuh thoughts?' asked Esme, flicking him a quick, anxious glance. 'Or mebbe they're the same as mine.'

'Mebbe they are at that,' murmured Clyde, his gaze flat and unblinking on the lifting glare of the early sun.

But were they, he wondered? All he had seen in Esme's eyes these past months had been her doubts of where the future lay; would there be a future out here with the homestead, the harsh, often unyielding land, the grinding work of the years ahead to make a living from the dust and dirt through seasons that seemed sometimes to give so little and always take so much?

Damn it, she was still young, flush of her womanhood, with a spirit of determination, courage, no shirking hard work and effort, with maybe her own thoughts of building something here for a family still to come and plan for. Years with her hands to the plough and the dirt, though, would take their own cruel toll.

And then he had seen the fear. There in the glazed, dazed look at the shooting of Sep Kline; there in the dread of riding to town for supplies under the taunting, leering gaze of Larsen and his men, and there last night in the torching of Charlie's barn, his vicious death, and lurking long and deep behind the sadness of comforting a grieving widow.

There too, damn it, in the sight of the man they had carted from the Utepan . . .

'First thing we're goin' to do is sort that fella,' said Clyde, his fingers tightening on the reins again. 'I want some answers. I wanna know who he is, why he's here and just why he's so concernin' Larsen — and just how it was he got himself shot so bad.'

'And when yuh got all this — if yuh do — what then?' asked Esme, tossing her hair to her shoulders.

'He'll have to go, no questionin' on it. We got enough trouble on our hands without harbourin' some personal feud 'tween him and Larsen. Can't stand in the middle of it, and that's a fact. He goes — best he can. Go find himself a doc or somethin'.'

'He still ain't in no fit state — ' began Esme.

'He just ain't our concern no more,' snapped Clyde, his gaze ahead hardening. 'We done our best by him, but there's other matters now a whole lot more pressin'. There's Charlie to bury decent, his woman and young 'uns to look to, stock and the land . . . Hell, we ain't got time for tendin' no has-been gunslinger, specially if he's locked in with Larsen somehow. No, Esme, he goes. I ain't for turnin' out no wounded man, no more I would an animal, but comes the time, comes the day . . . '

'And when he's gone?' said Esme, reining her mount to a sudden halt, her stare tight and fixed. 'When yuh turned out the fella, what yuh goin' to do then, Clyde? Yuh goin' to face Larsen, reckon on a siege, wait 'til we get burned out and I'm askin' the last man standin' if he'd spare the time to dig your grave? Or are we goin' to get to packin' and load that wagon we just fixed with a new wheel? Lucky we did if we're pullin' out!'

Clyde reined his mount to face her. 'That what yuh want?' he asked darkly. 'That the way yuh see it?'

'T'ain't a matter of what I want, is it? More a case of what I'm goin' to get if we don't reckon this for the best — for us, you and me, and a marriage we barely got started.'

'We pull out and there'll never be no settlin'. Damn it, Esme, there's a whole world of Larsens out there.'

'And just one right here, right now!'

They reined on, slow and easy to the gentle tinkle of tack and murmur of leather, the morning broken full and bright now, the first shimmering haze of the heat lifting like a flickering light.

'Figure for mebbe ridin' East,' said Clyde quietly. 'Get to them railroad company men and tell 'em how it is, try drillin' some sense into their heads. Hell, we got the law — '

'The fella's horse,' said Esme, swinging her mount ahead of Clyde as she raised a hand to shield her eyes, 'yuh move it from the corral?'

'No,' frowned Clyde, drawing alongside his wife. 'Been there since we brought the fella in.'

Esme's gaze swung across the line of the homestead fencing. 'T'ain't there now,' she croaked, urging her mount to a snorting gallop. 'in fact, it ain't nowhere to be seen!'

It needed no more than a fast, straight pace to clear the distance to the homestead paddock, dismount, hitch their mounts, for Clyde to scamper to the corral and then on to the barn and the small tack shed at the rear of it, and for Esme to pass almost as if in a daze to the living-room, its clutter untouched from the previous night's late supper, and step by soft, uncertain step reach the room where the man had lain for the past four days.

She paused, one hand on the jamb, her breath caught suddenly in the tightness of her throat, her eyes wide, mouth half open on sounds that stayed silent, and stared at the empty, crumpled bed, the bright red spots of fresh blood across the floorboards, the bared, stark hook in the wall where what remained of the man's clothes had hung.

'He's gone, just like that,' said Clyde at her back. 'Saddled up, ridden out, due north, an hour ago at most.' Esme heard his gulped swallow. 'And that gun's gone with him.'

When at last she turned from the deserted room it was only to stare into shadows that had not been there just a few short minutes ago.

5

She stripped the bed of the soiled linen, still warm to her touch where the man had lain, piled the pillows with the blankets in a heap, swept a besom across the floor of the room with a force and a venom that lifted the dust where none had been, tore down the frail, sun-faded drapes, attacked a pestering fly, chased a startled spider, and did not stop until the tears were dried to grey smudges on her hot, flaming cheeks and she fell back exhausted, breathless and drained.

'Darn fool!' croaked Esme to the empty room, her gaze round the space blurred on a haze of sweat and a well of fresh tears. 'Didn't have need to go. Shouldn't have. Won't get far, anyhow.' She groaned through a shuddering sigh, leaned on the wall and closed her eyes on the sting of their dampness. 'So just go bleed to death,' she murmured. 'See if I care!'

But she did, and she knew it, could feel it like a thudding ache in her head. Damn it, how did a fellow in that state get to even thinking he could ride out and stay saddled for more than a handful of miles? What was so vital that he should even reckon on it? Where would he go — to town, to find Larsen? Well, he could think again on that score! Sure, he could. Be in no shape to draw that custom-built, gunfighter's Colt, let alone fire it.

And he might at least have shown his gratitude, said something, anything, if only 'goodbye' . . .

Joe Medley expressed much the same feelings later that day when he sat his mount along of Clyde far out on the deserted, sunlit plain watching the last curls of smoke drift from the shell of Charlie Bishop's fire-gutted barn.

'Hard on Esme, all she did for him,' he had said, his soft gaze settled on the distant drift. 'Still, that's the way of it with his kind. Not giving a deal to anybody, save themselves. But no loss, Clyde. Longer yuh had him under yuh roof, worse it could have gotten for yuh, 'specially when Larsen got to hear. And he would, yuh can bet on it. Rat smells a rat, don't it? No, good riddance to my figurin', but he ain't goin' to make it far, is he? Not a deal to be found headin' north. Ten miles, fifteen if he's lucky before that wound starts bleeding again, and then . . . '

He had hissed softly through his lips. 'Tell yuh somethin', shan't be losin' no sleep over him and wouldn't lift a finger to him if he crawled by right now. He's on his own, wherever he is.'

Joe had sat quietly, his gaze still settled on the smoke, the soft, almost peaceful shimmer of it over the cloudless blue sky.

'Meantime, decent men die to no good purpose,' he had murmured, and then, with a furtive glance at Clyde, continued, 'Talked with the others, and we're agreed — we bury Charlie fittin', trail him into town, sun-up t'morrow. Take his rightful place on Boot Hill. Be a risk, but we figure not even Larsen havin' the spite to hold us back on a proper burial, 'specially with the womenfolk and young 'uns along of us. Charlie would want it that way. Feel it himself been you or me for Boot Hill.'

He had cleared his throat carefully. 'Which it might be, next time round,' he had added with a grunted bluntness. 'And before yuh say it, Clyde, we ain't for bein' persuaded no other against what we all decided: we start packin', pullin' out in the three weeks we got. Ain't nothin' else for it. Nothin' to be proud of, o'course, but there, that's the way of it when yuh got family. Can't stand to my kin bein' left. T'ain't in a man's nature.'

It had been another full minute then before Joe had grunted again, swung his gaze from the drifting smoke and reined away.

'Funeral wagons leave Charlie's place sun-up,' was all he had called.

Clyde had sat silent and alone on the plain for some time, his eyes almost unblinking on the dark, skeletal remains of the smouldering barn, his face without so much as a twitch or flicker of expression, his thoughts as charred and blackened as the burned-out heap.

'But yuh wrong, Joe,' he had finally murmured to himself against the glare of the high sun, 'decent men don't die to no good purpose. Not out here they don't.'

★　★　★

First light next day broke slow and smeared through a sweep of low cloud; a funereal light, fitting to the day, most had thought, as Charlie Bishop's body was sealed in the rough hewn coffin and placed reverently aboard the blanket-draped, low-sided wagon, picks and shovels along of it for the digging.

There had been few words exchanged between folk through that early hour as the freshening wind whipped at the

47

skirts of the women and raised a rosy glow on the scrubbed, polished cheeks of the Sabbath-suited youngsters. Only few whispered were for the grieving widow, between the men as they readied the wagon teams, settled the mounts, shushed young Sammy Keyes against playing his harmonica, Charlie's whining dog in its endless pacing.

'Mr Bishop goin' to Heaven?' asked a wide-eyed Sarah Medley, clutching at the brim of her bouncing hat as her pa lifted her to the womenfolk's wagon.

'You can bet on it,' said Joe with the merest flicker of a reassuring smile.

'Will God help him build a new barn?' frowned the youngster.

'You can bet on that too,' gulped Joe. 'Best there is.'

'I just hope so. Mr Bishop was a nice man. He deserves a new barn.'

Henry Keyes had reined his mount quickly to the head of the first team, taken up station alongside it, looked back, catching the gaze of Clyde Green as he did so, then nodded, raised an arm to the drivers, and urged the wagons forward to the trail.

'Never figured as how I'd see a day like this,' said Frank Cooper, rolling to the gentle pace of his mount at Clyde's side. 'Could just as easy get to spittin' as prayin'.'

'Prayin' comes first,' muttered Clyde, his eyes narrowing to a sudden whip of the wind. 'Spittin' can wait 'til this is done.'

'Mebbe,' sighed Frank. 'But not for me, Clyde. No, I guess not. Mite too old for fightin'. Kids growin' up there, gettin' to a time when they look to their pa for the way of things. And their ma wants for them to get to readin' and writin', make somethin' of themselves. Don't reckon for it bein' dirt-scratchin'.'

'Still your land out there, though,' said Clyde.

'Yeah,' croaked Frank with a slow, drifting glance to the cloud-shrouded plain, 'but for how much longer?'

They fell to silence as the wagons

creaked on, the wind whipped and the light shifted uneasily through the low morning sky. Stark, blackened ruins of the barn there, mournful wisp of smoke, said all that was needed, thought Clyde, wondering if somewhere deep in the lost grey lands, far beyond the homesteads and the town, the wounded gunfighter had finally come to his rest. No burial for him, no mourners, nobody there to say the last words, and no marker neither to say who he was.

But, then, nobody would ever need to know, would they?

* * *

Esme Green was pondering much the same thoughts as she hugged the shawl across her shoulders, flexed her fingers through the cold, anxious grip of the widow's hand, and balanced herself to the creak and grind of the trundling wagon.

Day was full of death, she thought,

gritting her teeth against a surge of anger. Charlie's body up there, stiff and sealed in crude pine planking, the gunfighter almost certainly dead and gathering flies like he was no more than yesterday's dung, and if death was not yet in bodies, it was sure as hell fast scrawling its lonely despair across the faces of those gathered round her.

Not a woman here who was not wondering how long before she too would be taking her place in the widow's seat, waiting on the touch of a hand, the murmured word, the nod, the glance; recalling the sounds, the shapes of her man just two days gone, the years not yet begun. Not a young one without an emptiness too bewildering to under-stand — and not an acre of land neither without that pinched grey look to its sprawling dirt.

Sun-up this day would be a long time coming, if anybody had a mind to notice, or even care.

She blinked on a whipping gust of the wind and settled her gaze on the bland morning shapes of the town in the distance. Quiet as a breath this time of day, nothing barely moving save for a lone dog slinking through the shadows, fading twist of smoke from the forge and livery, flicker of a lantern back of the Trailbender bar and eating-house, corner of a loose canvas caught on the wind, scattering of dust, swirl of dirt. Nobody about, not yet.

But how long before any one of the blank, staring windows there filled with a face and eyes that would blink their sleep clear in an instant?

She smiled fitfully as her husband reined ahead of the wagons to join Henry Keyes riding point.

'Town ain't for wakin' this early,' said Henry, his gaze steady and probing in its sweep of the main street and buildings.

'Give it two minutes,' murmured Clyde, his own gaze following Henry's. 'Don't take much to stir Larsen.'

Henry grunted and slid his fingers over the slackened reins. 'Takin' one helluva risk here, yuh know. Larsen might see it as baitin' him to the limit.'

'Doin' it to the book, though, ain't we? Funeral procession goin' about its duty as it should, sober and respectful, and not a gun between us, like we agreed. And damnit, Henry, we got a right to this. It's our town, our street up there. Our Boot Hill.'

'Didn't risk it for Sep, did we? Buried him out there on the plain.'

'So we did,' murmured Clyde again. 'And that was a mistake. Too runnin' scared to see it any other.'

'Yuh mean we ain't runnin' scared now?' mocked Henry, slanting his gaze to Clyde. 'Don't count me in on that, or yuh speakin' just for yourself?'

'I know yuh for better than that, Henry Keyes, so don't yuh go foolin' me none about — '

His voice and words slid away at the sight of the four figures slouching and scuffing their steps to the head of the street, pausing at the last stretch of a tumbledown store shed and settling

53

their stares like perching vultures on the approaching wagons.

'Larsen standin' to yuh right,' croaked Henry from a throat that had tightened in seconds.

'I see him,' said Clyde. 'Don't pay him no heed. Just keep goin'.'

'Now I *am* scared — and I *ain't* foolin'!'

6

The man had two legs, two arms, a body, head and shoulders, a sullen, ageless face, slanting eyes to a tight-lipped mouth, but most would not have reckoned for him being born of a natural mother.

Goff Larsen had been spawned some place deep, somewhere dark and lost, watched over, fed and nurtured by something not of this world and thrown to it as the runt of his batch. Some reckoned you could see it all in the strange, fish-like eyes — one coloured cold blue, the other washed green — others in the twist of his lips, the sound of that echoing voice that seemed always, whatever the hour, to be of the night.

But most never got too long to figuring. You got that close to Larsen, close enough for him to notice and not take kindly to the curiosity, and you were usually dead. Invariably dead. Inevitably so.

It was just the 'natural' way of things in Goff Larsen's other world.

So the secret, as on that chilled, cloudy, windswept morning on the trail to the main street into Mission, was not to catch the fellow's eye too soon, or not before you were forced. Or not at all if you laid any store to making it on, even though you were a funeral procession grey in its grief.

You had to remember that every day was a funeral day in Larsen's sight.

'Hold up there,' called a lean, long-legged sidekick stepping from Larsen's side, a Winchester cradled tight across his body. 'Yuh goin' some place?' he drawled, a grin spreading his tobacco stained lips.

'Don't rein up 'til we're real close,' hissed Clyde without shifting his gaze from the men. 'They can see we ain't armed.'

'Yuh figure that for making a

difference?' muttered Henry. 'Look on the faces of them scum — '

'Just do it, Henry!' snapped Clyde.

The sidekick eased his weight to one hip, recradled the rifle, hawked a fount of spittle to the dirt, and stared.

Larsen stayed silent, unmoving, his eyes seemingly sightless, hands deep in the pockets of his long dust-coat.

The wind snapped. A sliver of loose dirt wriggled across the lifeless ground. Clouds scudded.

'Well?' drawled the sidekick again as the wagons creaked to a halt. 'I asked a question.'

'Answer's right there,' said Clyde, nodding to the coffin. 'Charlie Bishop. Don't need no remindin', do yuh?'

Henry stiffened, a chill of sweat already at his shoulders as the sidekick spat again and ranged a tighter, sharper gaze from the coffin to the womenfolk, to Joe and Frank mounted back of the outfits, to Henry and then slowly, darkly, to Clyde where it stayed without blinking.

'Ain't no place here for sodbusters,' mouthed the man, flexing his fingers over the rifle stock.

'Place is Boot Hill and the time is now,' clipped Clyde. 'Be obliged if yuh'd show some respect and stand aside there.'

Henry stifled a moan and twitched his shoulders. A mount tossed its head. Tack jangled, leather creaked. 'Why have we stopped?' called Sarah Medley, craning from her mother's arms before being snaffled from sight. Clyde stiffened, stared and waited.

'You folk get Mr Larsen's message?' asked the man, his fingers still busy on the stock. 'Three weeks, that's all yuh got.' The stained grin flickered again. 'Wouldn't want for yuh to be wastin' time on more coffins, would we?'

'Only time pressin' is for this fella to be buried decent,' said Clyde, his gaze drifting from the sidekick to where Larsen waited, still unmoving, still with his stare as blank and hollow as a black hole on the thin morning light.

'Wouldn't take more than an hour at most,' flustered Henry, the sweat beading on his brow. 'Not that if we — '

'Let 'em pass,' growled a stockier, thicker-set man at Larsen's side. 'Get this done, and make it fast.'

'Well, that's real — ' began Henry again, but withered under Clyde's snap of reins and raised arm to the waiting drivers.

Wagon timbers ached to the heave of horses, hoofs scuffed, wheels squeaked and groaned into motion, the youngsters squirmed, the wind flapped at bonnets and skirts, pale faces drained to an ashen grey and Widow Bishop sobbed uncontrollably into her hands.

Henry was about to mouth 'Obliged', but made no more than a choking grunt as the procession trundled on to the street.

Sarah Medley pulled a face at the rifle-toting sidekick and gripped the brim of her bouncing, floppy-brimmed hat.

'Said as how the sonofabitch

wouldn't interfere, didn't I?' muttered Joe to Frank Cooper. 'Even Larsen ain't got the stomach for messin' with a fella's funeral.'

'Who says he ain't?' said Frank with a hurried glance back to the watching men. 'We ain't buried Charlie yet, and we sure as hell ain't *left* town!'

Joe simply swallowed and slumped to a chilled silence as the street closed in and the dusty drift of the dirt track to Boot Hill darkened under a scud of cloud.

★   ★   ★

Esme Green sighed and shivered, shuffled her legs in the folds of her skirt, tapped her numbed toes into life and stared for a moment into the blurred and shaded shapes of that hang-dog morning. She brushed at a speck of rain at her cheek, shivered again and wondered if she dare close her eyes.

It might be too soon to try; perhaps

Larsen's staring eyes would still be there, just as they had through the minutes of the wagons waiting to pass to the street, that dead, hollow-eyed look never leaving her, not so much as blinking, only devouring, eating into her like some slow, sucking slug boring deep into her head. The look of a man who touched and felt and fondled with his stare.

She flinched, shrugged and reached for the hand of the widow, her fingers working anxiously for her own grip of reassurance. But nothing, she thought, coming sharply to an awareness of the town and street, had been said or asked of the gunfighter. So had Larsen given up on him, dismissed him; was he still waiting on him, or worse had he already found him, blood-soaked and exhausted, and put him out of his misery?

Or had the gunfighter finally come to his senses and held hard and fast to the wild trail north?

Hell, did it matter?

She flinched again at the trundling creak of the wagon, conscious now of the townfolk lining the board-walks, their faces empty, eyes watchful, not a limb moving, not a sound made. Storekeeper Cartwright, with his hands buried deep in his apron; Doc McLean, his thatch of white hair straggling on the wind; Sheriff Tamms, his face as haunted as ever in the grip of his guilt, the shame of his impotence at the guns of Larsen; Ship O'Toole, straddling the steps of his saloon, cigar already lit and glowing, his Trailbender girls hovering like a dance of butterflies round him; the youths, the young ones, old-timers and worn, hard-grafting women — until, as the street petered out to the track, there was only the livery and the shirt-sleeved bulk of blacksmith, Billhook, and the creeping twists of smoke at his forge.

That was Mission, thought Esme, a simple town, home to simple folk, destined one day to be the biggest, busiest, wealthiest rail-head this side of the Utepan. No place for sodbusters.

She sighed again as the wagons creaked to a halt on the bleak, windswept slopes of Boot Hill. Maybe Charlie Bishop would get to looking down on the town in the years to come and figure it for what it might have been. Or maybe, if they found a spot for him top of the hill, he would see clear and straight to the land he once farmed.

Be a railroad by then, so maybe he would just sleep.

★ ★ ★

They had dug Charlie's grave, lowered the coffin to it, Clyde Green saying the words as he saw fitting, all paid their respects in their manner, little ones included, and replaced the earth, packed neat and smoothed to a careful mound, in a little short of two hours.

There was a fine drizzle drifting on the chilled air by then.

The townfolk had watched, silent,

respectful — or maybe too scared to do much else, Joe had thought — from a distance, some gathered in grey, sullen groups, some standing apart, some, Ship O'Toole among them, with scant patience or regard for the proceedings. Sheriff Tamms had retreated to the darkest corner of the boardwalk, storekeeper Cartwright shuffled his hands in his apron, Billhook left his forge to stand, bare-headed, bare-armed, a hammer still gripped in one hand, at the foot of the slope as if, Clyde had thought, in a personal token of defiant respect. For the others, there had been only hollow stares, tight mouths, barely the shift of a boot in the dirt.

Larsen and his sidekicks — grown to a dozen now — had stayed close, equally watchful, almost as silent, save for the hawking, the spitting, the tapping on loose cradled rifles, the butts of low-holstered Colts.

'Done the best I can here,' said Frank, bringing the simple marker to the head of the grave. 'T'aint as I wanted, but there ain't been the time.'

'Looks fine,' said Joe, as he ran the tip of a finger over the poker-burned wording. ' 'Charlie Bishop' he read aloud. ' 'Good man. Good Farmer' Couldn't have said it better. Guess that's how we all feel.'

'What we all know, that's for sure,' murmured Frank. 'What the folk hereabouts should be knowin' if they'd a grain of sense between 'em, the guts to stand t'gether, get to shiftin' — '

'Steady there, Frank,' soothed Clyde. 'This ain't the time.'

'Good a time as any. Don't get no closer to speakin' the truth than when a fella's steppin' up to his Maker!' Frank's voice lifted a pitch as his gaze, tight and fiery now, slid across the mourners to the townfolk and the lounging sidekicks. 'Know what we written here!' he shouted.

'Frank . . . ' hissed Clyde, reaching for the man's arm.

'Well, I'll tell yuh. We said here as

how Charlie Bishop was a good man. And that he was. Good husband to his widow there and them young 'uns she got to her skirts. Good pa, a God-fearin', decent-livin' fella . . . Yuh hear that?'

'Frank, f'Cris'sake!' hissed Clyde again, glancing anxiously at the side-kicks.

'He farmed his land good, too. Bent his back, worked his hands 'til they bled. And for what? Well, in case yuh ain't heard it proper, if nobody here ain't got to tellin' the real truth of it . . . '

'Frank!' growled Clyde. 'Not here. Not like this.'

'Truth of it,' bellowed Frank, raising the marker high above his head. 'Truth is — '

The shot blazed loud and fast, as if in the crack and spit of forked lightning, splintering the marker in Frank's hand, ripping it from his grip to slither it across the newly dug dirt, down the dusty slope to the feet of a wide-eyed, hushed group of townswomen.

'Get the hell out of it, sodbuster,' cursed the long-legged sidekick striding to the hill, the Winchester ranging menacingly. 'Out now before yuh get to join that corpse there!'

Frank had fallen back under Clyde's anxious tugging; Joe Medley turned with Henry Keyes to protect the cringing mourners, whimpering youngsters. The blacksmith made a move towards the oncoming sidekick, Doc McLean settled his hat firmly on his head, and Sheriff Tamms scurried into the depths of his office when the second shot screeched like the call of a strangled hawk from somewhere beyond Larsen and the watching townsfolk, in the deepest darkness of that grey, clouded morning.

A single shot that lifted the long-legged sidekick clean from his feet and tossed him to the dirt with a thud that seemed to shudder to the very foundations of that fearful town.

The silence seemed to hang then like a shroud.

7

Esme Green watched the lantern glow flicker over the faces of the women huddled in hushed conversation at the far end of the homestead veranda, the youngsters snuggled to them, heard the night wind in its eerie whistle through the shadowed paddock, the soft snort of a horse, creak of timber, and was a long time daring to lift her gaze to the moon and the still troubled clouds scudding across it.

Skies up there looked as haunted, grey and cold as she felt. She shivered, tightened the shawl across her shoulders and into her neck, and smiled softly into the staring eyes of Sarah Medley.

How did you get to explaining to an eight year old what had happened today back there in town, she wondered? Where did you begin that would make any sense? Where were the words?

She lifted a hand for the youngster to come to her, held her close in her skirts, and turned her gaze slowly to the brighter light beyond the open door to the living-room where Clyde and the others were gathered round the table, their voices lifting, falling, sometimes no more than whispers, sometimes sharp and growling, tumbling and jostling among themselves like slivers of grit in a landfall.

'Say what yuh like, any way yuh like, but somebody — God alone knows who — pulled a trigger t'day against Larsen. That ain't happened since the sonofabitch set foot in this territory. And nobody, not a soul, saw a damn thing.' Henry Keyes leaned back in the chair at the head of the table and folded his arms.

'Somebody fired a shot, sure they did, but who, f'Cris'sake?' said Joe Medley, his eyes wide and bulging. 'Who'd have the guts for it?'

'That gunfighter fella we dragged in

from the 'Pan — he'd have the guts and mebbe good reason too,' murmured Frank Cooper, circling an empty tin mug over the surface of the table.

'But what yuh sayin' there?' frowned Henry. 'Yuh sayin' as how the fella rode outa here in the state he was in, holed up some place in town or close by, waitin' on his chance of settin' about Larsen and his sidekicks? We talkin' retribution of some kind? That what yuh sayin'? Hell, that takes some believin'! That fella was bleedin', mebbe carryin' lead buried deep, more than like fevered up. How would a man in that state — '

'We know Larsen has a real concern over the fella — that sidekick said as much to Esme — so mebbe he's expectin' him, knows for a fact he's close. Who's to say what gets to squirmin' when fellas of their kind crawl outa the dark?' Frank steadied the mug and lifted his gaze. 'One helluva shot, though, ain't he?' he grinned cynically.

'Still takes some swallowin',' sighed Joe.

'Tell yuh what yuh should be swallowin' on,' grimaced Henry. 'Yuh should be figurin', like yuh ain't never figured before, where all this leaves us. Yuh thought of that? Well, I have, the hell I have!'

He paused a moment, the light flickering at the sweat on his brow, spreading the shadows across one cheek. 'We were lucky to get clear of town t'day in one piece. Not that Larsen had a deal of choice. Wouldn't get to shootin' the lot of us front of the whole town, and mebbe he was too stunned to bother. But what happens when he gets to thinkin' straight again? What then? We still goin' to have three weeks, or are we lookin' at three days? Or do we start pullin' out right now, this minute?' He paused again. 'Who's goin' to pay for the shootin' of that sidekick?'

'We ain't, not if we get organized,' said Clyde quietly, easing slowly to the table from the deeper shadows. 'No sayin' just how Larsen's reactin' right now, but one thing he ain't doin' is scurryin' round town like a spooked fly lookin' for the hand behind that shot. T'ain't his style. Too smart for that. No, he'll wait, let the man make the next move, button that town down 'til it ain't barely breathin'. Nobody'll spit save on Larsen's say so. Nobody lift a finger, take a step outa place. He'll want Mission closed up, a prison — with himself the governor and his men the warders. And that suits us just fine.'

'Tell me how yuh reckon that,' grunted Henry.

'We're mebbe buyin' some time here,' said Clyde. 'No sayin' how long, but long enough for me to do what I should've done way back: get to them legal fellas, land agents and the real law back East. Three days' ride to Carver City; there and back inside a week with help and some sanity ridin' along of me.'

He settled his hands on the table and leaned forward to gaze long and hard into the eyes watching him.

'And you, the three of yuh, will stay here, look to the women and the young 'uns with yuh lives,' he added calmly, bluntly. 'Anybody sets a foot on this land who ain't the right to be here, yuh kill 'em, right there, no messin'.' Clyde came back to his full height, his gaze hardened now to a glinting stare. 'I ain't a notion who pulled that trigger t'day, and I ain't for no wild guessin'. All I know for certain is that Sep Kline and Charlie Bishop didn't die for nothin'. I ain't goin' to let that happen, and neither are you, are yuh?'

Esme stiffened at the sudden clutch of the girl at her hip.

'Will it all be better t'morrow, Mrs Green?' mumbled Sarah.

Where were the words then to reassure, she wondered, her gaze reaching Clyde's without either of them daring to speak?

Clyde Green had saddled up, loose-roped a trail mount as a spare, packed for the three-day ride to Carver, and was making his final checks an hour before the first hint of breaking light in the grey sprawl to the east.

'Bad weather's breaking,' he murmured, his back to Esme as he adjusted his saddle girth yet again. 'Dry and hot come noon.' He paused, his hands still and sweaty to the chill touch of the leather. 'Should make good time . . . ' He turned sharply, his look intense, unblinking on Esme's pale, drawn face. 'Yuh ain't much for this, are yuh?' he said softly, his voice cracked and breaking.

'Is it right?' asked Esme, her fingers fumbling through the fringed edges of the shawl. 'This the only way?'

'Can't see no better. If we don't get to them lawmen in Carver — '

'I know, I heard yuh,' sighed Esme, her stare flat on the shadowed land

74

beyond the paddock.

Clyde laid a hand on her arm, drew her close and folded his arms round her. 'T'ain't been much for yuh, has it? Two years wed and a half of that spent fightin' for a hold on what we got here. Not a deal goin' for us in married life, eh? Couldn't blame yuh if yuh — '

Esme snuggled closer. 'That's fool talk, Clyde Green, and yuh know it,' she whispered, a tear spilling to his shirt.

'Mebbe, mebbe . . . But damn it, I ain't for throwin' in my hand yet. Can't do that, Esme, not for you, not for m'self, not for the others. There's gotta be a way.' He broke from the closeness and stood back. 'Henry, Joe, Frank, they'll look to yuh 'til I'm back. Got their word on it.'

'You just look to y'self, yuh hear?' said Esme, brushing at another tear. 'Two years wed and we ain't got started yet!' She smiled quickly on the tremble of her lips. 'Get y'self back here . . . '

'You bet,' grunted Clyde, mounting

up and reining the horse to the northern trail. 'Skirt the Utepan out there, then take the hill track; Renegade Creek, Cloud Top drift, straight through to Carver. Three days at most. Two and a lick if I get lucky.'

'Stay lucky!' grinned Esme. She took the reins at the mount's head. 'That shootin',' she said, her face drawn and pale again, the tearstains streaked and bright on her cheeks in the shifting gloom. 'Could it have been ...? I mean, is there any chance it might have been the stranger? Nobody saw anythin', but just supposin' — ?'

'Sound that shot made over that distance — only one gun that good: long-barrelled Peacemaker.'

'That what the man was carryin'?'

'The very same,' said Clyde, tightening the reins. 'Sound yuh don't f'get once heard.' He half turned the mount to the trail. 'Won't have escaped Larsen. Wonder how many times he's heard it before?'

How many times might he hear it

again, wondered Esme, as she watched her man clear the paddock and waited to catch his last wave before rider and mount and the trailing packhorse were a fading blur on the slow early light?

8

He cleared the main drift of the parched Utepan trail, riding far to the west of its scorched, sizzling heart — the Badlands where men died slow on the madness of thirst — and was heading fast for the first lift of rock and boulders to Renegade Creek by the time the noon sun was high and the land a shimmering haze.

Steady pace from here, he reckoned, keep the horses fresh for the long haul through the Creek. Should make the southern mouth of it well before nightfall; then rest and water up, eat cold, no fire, sleep best he could. Clear the Creek and set a livelier pace for Cloud Top; maybe take the higher route; rough going in parts, but a saving of a half-day if he stayed wide awake and concentrated.

Mounts were looking good, air was a

deal fresher and thinner after the rain; would take a whole day to get to its stifling peak again. So far, then, so good, and not a stick of a problem to fret him.

Save those he had left behind.

Asking some of Esme to be there at the homestead by herself, not that he was doubting for a moment that Frank and the others would look to her, sun-up, noon, sundown, and manage the stock too. Even so . . . Took the best of the nerve out of him to leave her like that. Hell, it took more than nerve for Esme to stand there and watch him go! Some woman. But, then, he had known that for sure minute he had set eyes on her that day in Marton.

Still left him bewildered, though, to think she had accepted his offer of marriage, put the neat, trim store life with her ma and pa behind her and made the long journey out West.

And to what?

Hell, no point in dwelling on that at a time like this. Fact was, their land, their whole livelihood, was under threat; Sep Kline and Charlie Bishop were dead, and there were widows' weeds where there should have been grazing and crops.

There was also Larsen.

There was the man who had fired that shot back there on Boot Hill.

There was perhaps the nameless, faceless gunfighter, still alive and breathing, still here some place for whatever reasons had brought him this way all those days back.

There was fear too. Among the homesteaders — every face showed it — and right there in Mission among folk pitched to the mayhem and haunting of a dread they could not fathom, much less had the guts to call to a showdown.

And there was still Larsen. There was always Larsen.

But there had been that blazing single shot, the echo of it still ringing in Clyde's ears even now. Whose hand on the gun, whose eye behind the aim, whose finger on the trigger?

Only one gun had a roar like that.

Clyde had been the one to find it in the scorched dirt of the Utepan, at the side of a man they had taken for dead . . .

It was the tugging drag of the rope to the packhorse, the sudden snort and slither of hoofs over loose shale and rock that scratched across Clyde's thoughts and brought him to a jangling halt.

'Easy there, easy,' he soothed, half turning in the saddle to the pack as it tossed its head in a frenzy of wild, bulging eyes.

Rattler close by, animal on the prowl through the shade, he wondered, peering hard now for some slithering movement, a hungry padding? Nothing he could see, nothing to smell neither, he thought, sniffing on the lean air.

He dismounted, gathered the rope through his hands as he approached the pack and might easily have missed the movement on the drift of a ridge, had the horse not shaken its head again.

Somebody out there, he reckoned, squinting against the glare. Shape of a rider, and maybe more than one, judging by the way the shadows had split before disappearing into cover.

Drifters heading for Carver, couple of travelling ranch hands heading for the cattle country plains beyond Cloud Top? Not too many took to this trail of choice. Deal longer but a darn sight easier to hold to the tracks to the east . . .

And then a Winchester barked and Clyde Green hit the dirt with a squirming thud.

★   ★   ★

He was still flat on the ground, dirt between his teeth, across his tongue, his eyes blinking on dust, when he heard the crunch of approaching boots.

Worn, creased leather, soles that had seen better days . . . steps that slowed, scuffed, settled . . . legs parted in a stance that straddled . . . a shadow, thick and tall, falling across him like a watching cloud.

More steps, another pair of boots, same worn leather, same scuffing crunch, until the shadows merged and the glare of the day was blotted out.

Clyde blinked again, swallowed the gritty dirt, and waited, listening to the men's hollow breathing, the oozing slap of one of them chewing on cheap baccy, the grunt and then the long, resigned sigh.

'Well, now,' came the voice, rough and parched, 'if it ain't the sodbustin' Mr Green. Yuh see this, Eli? Yuh see what we got ourselves here?'

The second man chuckled and spun a sliver of dirt over Clyde's head with the toe of his boot.

'Mite distanced from yuh patch, ain't yuh, mister?' came the voice again. 'Yuh goin' some place? Seems like it, pack horse along of yuh there. Now where would that be? Not all the way to Carver City, would it, by any chance?

Hell, what yuh wanna go there for?'

Clyde screwed his eyes on the swirl of more dirt, flinched at the prod in his ribs.

'On yuh knees, mister,' snapped the voice as the boots crunched back a step and the barrel of the Winchester glinted in the sunlight.

Clyde eased slowly from the ground, shuffled to his knees, reached for his hat, only to see it booted beyond his grasp.

'Lucky I didn't put that shot clean through yuh. Lucky I ain't figurin' on doin' just that right now. Be one helluva feast for them buzzards circlin' there, wouldn't yuh?'

A pock-faced, lizard-eyed fellow with a voice like the slop of dirty water in a rusted pail, noted Clyde, squinting into the face of the man staring down at him. The second man of a similar cut, he thought, save for the dribbling saliva at the corners of his mouth and the left eye hooded on a drooping lid that hung like a creased drape over the white of the ball behind it.

Larsen's men, no mistaking them; seen the pair of them hovering at the man's side back there in Mission. Smelled like Larsen's men too, he thought, spitting the dirt carefully from his tongue.

'Know somethin', mister?' said Pock-face, beginning to circle. 'Mr Larsen reckoned as how yuh might try somethin' like this. Said it straight out, he did. 'That fella Green'll head for Carver', he said. And yuh know somethin' else, mister? He weren't one mite happy with the thought. Nossir, not a lick-spit, he weren't. So we're here to see as how yuh don't. Simple as that.'

Hooded-eye chuckled and wiped his fingers through the dribbling saliva.

'Now, we pretty much got a free hand on the doin' of this,' continued Pock-face. 'Mr Larsen ain't much fussed just so long as it's done. But my good friend, Eli, here, well, he's come up with somethin' truly fittin' considerin' the performance you sod-busters put on there at Boot Hill. So . . . ' The man halted and ground the heels of his boots into the dirt. 'We brought along a shovel for yuh to dig yuh own grave right here, and when it's done, know what, we'll shoot yuh through so's yuh drop neat as a bug clean into it.' He grinned, spat and cleared a mottling of sweat from his cheeks. 'How's that suit yuh, Mr-sodbuster-Green? Yuh figure that's fittin' enough?'

Clyde swallowed and shuffled on his knees. 'Yuh seem to be callin' the shots,' he croaked. 'May as well get to it.'

Hooded-eye giggled. 'Ain't he just somethin'?' he squeaked.

'Ain't he?' grunted Pock-face, his stare darkening. 'Go get the shovel, Eli. We're wastin' good time here. Fella as keen as this to get to his grave shouldn't be kept waitin' on it.'

9

The sweat was burning on his bare back, trickling in hot, slithering channels across his shoulders, dripping to the dirt from his chin, blinding his eyes till they stung to no more than a squint on the salty bite. His hands were fixed and tight, manacled it seemed, to the handle of the shovel as he bent and lifted through the monotonous effort of digging his own grave; going ever deeper, inch by inch, foot by foot, standing waist-deep now in the yawning hole, hardly daring to shift his gaze to the grinning, slavering faces watching him.

No telling what fool thing he might get to doing if he caught their glares and his blood came to the boil faster than the lathering of his sweat.

He gulped and groaned to another scrape, another lift, another tossing of dirt to the growing heap above him, and winced on the sickening twist of his guts, the surge of half-crazed, jumbled thoughts through his mind.

Esme, the homestead, the land back there . . . faces of friends, the living-room, lantern glow at the supper-table after a long day's toil . . . the closeness, warmth of a body snuggled to him through the hours till sun-up . . . Esme in her one best dress at the Christmas hoe-down, the one she had worn on her wedding day. The death-streaked stare of Larsen . . . the half-dead gunfighter sprawled on the bed . . . Boot Hill, the confused, screaming voices . . .

'Now don't yuh get to slackin' none there, fella,' drawled Pock-face from the shadow of an outcrop of boulders. 'We ain't got the time. Just keep diggin'. I'll tell yuh when yuh gone deep enough.'

Hooded-eye giggled and slapped his lips on a spit of stained tobacco juice. 'Yuh gettin' thirsty there?' he squeaked. 'Hand yuh my canteen, save as how it don't seem worth the bother, does it, yuh goin' so soon to yuh Maker? Be a waste. Taught good by my ma not to go wastin' water.'

Surprised to hear you ever had one, thought Clyde, swinging the sweat from his face as he bent back to the hole. He gulped again, the saliva thick as syrup in his throat, and wondered how long he could drag this out. How long, more like, before Larsen's scum got bored, impatient to be out of the searing sun, back in the saddle, heading for Mission and the high praise and handouts from Larsen.

But drag it out to what, even if he could, he wondered; to making a break for it, chancing his arm on a sudden dash? Across open land, with the sun full up and no more than a handful of boulders for cover? Risk making it as far as his mount there, grab his rifle from its scabbard, blaze all the lead his trigger finger could pull on 'til he lay in a pool of his own blood with only the buzzards up there getting anxious?

Make a fight of it, any sort of fight,

when the time came for him to stand on the brink of his own grave waiting for the fatal shot, the final drop?

Hell, it had all been a terrible, pointless waste! Maybe he should have figured for Larsen reckoning on the homesteaders making a desperate move against the three-week deadline. Maybe he should have known the sonofabitch would be reading the situation from every angle, figuring on all the deals left for the homesteaders to play, their last fling in a bid to reach Carver City.

Maybe, too, he should have figured for himself that the shooting on Boot Hill would have set Larsen's mind to working through the darkest possibilities, chances he could not take, risks best avoided.

But from here on, when Clyde Green was no more than crow meat for whatever crawled into this hole, what then: what of Esme, the home, the others, the land they had given their lives for? What if . . .

'Say one thing for sodbusters,'

squeaked Hooded-eye again, 'they sure dig a mean hole.'

'Second nature, ain't it?' croaked out Pock-face. 'Shiftin' dirt, day in, day out. Should feel right at home down there, dead or alive!' The man came to his feet, fingers tapping over the butt of his Colt, and strolled casually to the head of the grave. 'Deep enough for yuh, mister?' he drawled. 'Yuh wanna try it for size? Wouldn't want yuh bein' uncomfortable down there. Goin' to be a long-time permanent resident, aren't yuh?'

Clyde spat, gripped the shovel, peered through sweat-soaked eyes. One swing of the shovel from here and he might . . .

'We all through here?' said Hooded-eye, shifting himself upright. 'We get to it now? Got me a gal waitin' back there in town.'

'Sure, we're through.' Pock-face's grin spread like a seeping pool of black water. 'Out yuh get, fella, nice and easy.'

Clyde eased himself painfully, slowly

from the grave as the men stood back, Colts drawn now, stances straddled over the shimmering dirt.

'Could've been a whole lot different for yuh, fella, yuh done what Larsen asked of yuh first place and gotten off yuh land,' said Pock-face, the gun shifting like a shadow in his grip. 'Spent all that time ploughin' and sowin' and mowin', and you with a young wife not yet broke full in — '

'Go to hell!' sneered Clyde. 'Go to hell and rot in it!'

'Say now, the fella's latherin' up,' squeaked Hooded-eye. 'Ain't it always the same when a man comes to it? Ain't they always got to get to the cursin' and moanin', and then there's the whimperin' kind. My, don't they just try a fella's patience some, 'specially when they — '

The buzzards wheeled in a squawking, squealing mass, a blot on the sky as menacing as a rain cloud; dirt lifted as if spat from some monster's mouth below the surface; Pock-face groaned,

92

clutching at a sudden surge of blood across his chest; Hooded-eye twisted, his half gaze glazed, mouth open on a flood of tobacco juice and foaming saliva, a hole, dark and deep and crimson, shot clean through the middle of his brow; and Clyde Green hit the ground again with a thud that rattled his ribs and pounded the breath from his throat as he watched Larsen's men slide slowly, almost silently, into the grave and lie there in a bleeding heap of twisted arms and straddled legs.

The high pitch and blaze of the roaring gunfire was fading to an echo when he dared to blink, risk the slightest movement and ease himself from the dirt, the clearing dust cloud, and squint across the land — to the left, the right, the long sprawl of it at his back.

But there was nothing, not a speck that moved or seemed it might, not a shadow out of place. Only the shimmering emptiness to distant, unmarked horizons.

'What the hell . . . ' croaked Clyde, spinning round again, sweat flying from his face as he struggled to widen his gaze against the glare. 'Who . . . ? Where . . . ?'

He gulped on a deadened throat, staggered to the shade of the boulders for Hooded-eye's canteen, swamped the water to his mouth, across his cheeks and scorched, blistering body, until he stood dripping sweat and tepid water in equal measure.

That gunfire, he thought, wiping his face, smearing the dust and damp to grey streaks, no mistaking it; the same roar, same pitch he had heard on the morning of the funeral. Peacemaker gunfire. The gunfighter, out here — God alone knew how — but here, and now, damn it, nowhere!

He kicked at the dirt, collected his shirt, hat, his gunbelt, holstered Colt, crossed to his mount, the pack horse and the standing horses of the sidekicks, then paused, one boot already to the stirrup.

Was he going on? Was it still worth the effort of reaching Carver? Dare he, when he knew now without the slightest lick of a doubt that Larsen would strike again once he realized he had seen the last of Pock-face and his partner — and this time with his sights set clear on the homesteads, the folk there, Esme?

What price was he prepared to pay for the frail hope of summoning help out of Carver?

What price had the gunfighter been prepared to pay to be here, to do what he had for a fellow no better than a lone-riding sodbuster?

Who was the piper; who called the tune?

Clyde Green had mounted up and left that place on the trail due North into Renegade Creek with no more than a sidelong glance at the grave he had dug for himself, and was already a disappearing shape and a fading sound when a tall man sitting a dark mare headed from that same empty land in the opposite direction.

Clyde was frowning, twisting his shoulders against the rub of his shirt across burned flesh, his thoughts teeming again through a nightmare escaped and the half-dozen that might yet slip their lairs, his head filled with the echoing pitch of gunfire, the sounds of the mocking sidekicks, scrape of the shovel, the slow slither of dead bodies to another man's grave.

The tall man on the dark mare was smiling softly to himself.

★ ★ ★

Esme Green had barely raised the flicker of a smile since sun-up. She had gone about her daily chores, from the mundane to the particular, as if in a trance, her fingers fluttering where they should have gripped, gripping where they should have simply brushed and passed on lightly.

She had stepped a dozen times and more from the living-room to the veranda to stare beyond the paddock to the far horizon on an empty land, seeing nothing, anxious only that the land was there, the horizon waiting; told herself as many times there was no point to staring — Clyde would be long beyond the Utepan by now, maybe as far as the Creek, planning his trail to Cloud Top, intent, concentrated and not looking back.

Still, she had convinced herself, no harm in just looking.

Henry Keyes had ridden in mid-morning, tended the stock, replenished the wood pile, assured, reassured, a firm arm across her shoulders, and left.

Joe Medley's wife had reckoned on raising Esme's spirits with a meat and potato pie cooked special for her. 'Yuh know how Nancy is,' Joe had smiled. 'Always figures on settlin' the nerve with a good meal. That's how I got this paunch!'

Frank Cooper, having taken charge of the Bishop spread, had passed through with Charlie's widow riding along of him on the buckboard. 'We're all thinkin' to yuh, Esme,' he had said, sampling the drink of cool lemonade with relish on a slap of his satisfied lips. 'Clyde, too,' he had added softly through a long gaze to the horizon. 'Sendin' my eldest boy, Nate, to look to yuh come sundown. He's a good lad, got a head on his shoulders. Yuh want for him to stay the night? Only got to say. He'll be happy enough sleepin' out here on the porch.'

But, no, Esme thought not; no need to go to such trouble, not yet. Maybe later.

Frank had nodded, said as how Joe would be by again at first light, the widow Bishop laid a hand to Esme's arm, and then they too had left and the day drifted, hot and bright, to the thickening gloom of an evening filled only with the company of clicking cicadas.

It was close on midnight, the air still heavy and sultry, when Esme turned down the glow of the lantern to a mere flicker, unbuttoned her dress to the waist, and crossed to bolt and secure the door.

She would try to sleep, she thought, leastways rest on the bed best her tumbling thoughts and the cluttering images would permit. A few short hours to another sun-up, another day, more chores she had no mind to, more of watching the empty lands, the long horizon.

She had the door almost closed when the boot thudded to the floor between it and the jamb and she stumbled back, a half cry squeezed to whimper in her throat, her eyes wide and staring, and the sudden cold chill of a sweat prickling at her neck.

She backed slowly to the table, her fingers fumbling a tin mug to a clattering spin across the boards, one hand reaching for a grip, her body tensing until it seemed something would crack.

The door swung open slowly on a surge of the night's blackness, the twinkling brightness of a cluster of stars, and creaked to a halt on its weathered hinges.

Esme waited, shuddering, her hands straying over the unbuttoned dress, fingertips brushing her parched lips, her stare frozen now on the dark space, dreading the shape that would fill it.

The soft, easy shift of a boot. The sound of deep breathing. Wafting smell of worn, unwashed clothes and the body beneath them.

Another step, the murmured creak of its careful measure.

And then the shadow, a dark, flexing claw reaching from the night to the flickering light and the shivering shape caught like a moth in its glow.

'Don't make a sound, lady, not if yuh wanna live.'

The voice was a hiss, the grin a twisted slit over broken teeth, the man's stare sharp and searing as a flame on Esme's face, her neck, the shaking limbs and body.

The man stepped closer, the grin

sprawling hungrily as two partners fell in behind him and folded their arms.

'Yuh got an appointment. Tonight, with Mr Larsen. Shall we go, real quiet?'

10

'She's gone, ain't she? And not of her own choosin' neither, so we don't get to debatin' who's done it, do we? Damn it, yuh can still smell the scum!'

Joe Medley crossed the living-room of the Green homestead to the table, slapped his hands firmly on its surface, and leaned forward, his gaze dark and angered. 'Only thing we got to ask ourselves is, what we goin' to do about it?' he growled, his eyes flicking from Henry Keyes' face to the grey empty stare of Frank Cooper.

'Should've reckoned on it,' murmured Henry.

'Well, mebbe we should have,' said Joe, 'but fact is we didn't, so ain't no point to thrashin' round it.'

'Should've insisted on my boy stayin' for the night,' grunted Frank, clenching his fingers to tight fists.

'Good thing yuh didn't,' said Joe again. 'Would've been another body for the hill if yuh had. Larsen's rats weren't here for messin'. Grab Esme and ride — any fool in the way was a dead man.'

'What they goin' to do with her?' shuddered Henry.

'Want me to spell it out?' Frank's fingers broke from the fists and flattened on the table. 'Yuh don't, do yuh?'

Joe left the table and strode to the open door, his gaze softening again on the morning light, the lifting dazzle of the sun. 'She's hostage against our shiftin', ain't she? Larsen'll hold her 'til we're gone. We sit it out, he'll kill her — piece by piece, knowin' him.' He turned sharply. 'And yuh can bet a fly to a heap of dung they've taken care of Clyde. How far did he get before a couple of Larsen's sidekicks picked him off? Ten miles if he was lucky.'

Henry groaned and hung his head. 'Yuh right, Joe, that's the way of it. And I wouldn't give a stick for Esme's life whatever we do. If Larsen don't get to finishin' her, she'll sure as hell be wishin' he had.'

The three drifted to an uncomfortable, fidgeting silence.

'They must've been watchin',' croaked Frank, staring into space. 'Every move, everythin' we did. Just waitin' on their chance.'

''Course they were watchin',' snapped Joe. 'Same as they are now, waitin' on seein' what we're goin' to do. Waitin' on us hittin' that trail into town.'

'We goin' to do that?' asked Henry, lifting his gaze from the table.

Joe turned his back on the first, flashing glare of the sunlight. 'Well, are we?'

Another moment of fidgeting silence, save for the tick of a clock, the tap of a finger, half stifled sigh.

'What about that gunfighter?' said Henry.

Joe thrust his hands to his trousers pockets and blinked wearily. 'What about him? He ain't here now, is he, ain't sittin' along of us? This ain't his fight. T'ain't his woman taken. Chances are he's cleared town, if he was ever there, got himself holed-up some place he can lick his wounds. Or die.'

'Ain't got to Larsen, has he?' frowned Frank.

Joe blinked again. 'And that ain't our affair neither. Our affair is — '

'Yeah, yeah, we hear yuh, Joe,' sighed Henry. 'Fact is, though, we gotta think this through.'

'Yuh ain't sayin' as how we're goin' to leave Esme to them rats, are yuh?' flared Joe, stepping deeper into the room. 'Yuh ain't thinkin' — '

'*Yuh'd better not be!*'

The voice from the veranda cracked like the splintering of new timber.

The men's heads turned as one, gazes wide, mouths opening, closing on tight swallows as the women gathered in the doorway eased a fraction closer, the young ones clutching at their skirts, shuffling uncertain feet.

'We ain't for none of that talk,' said Nancy Medley, settling her arms defiantly across her thrusting bosom, then nodding to the murmurs of Rosie Keyes and Megan Cooper. 'We been listenin' out here and we figure we got a say in this, seein' as how it's Esme you're discussin'.'

'Ain't no discussion necessary,' said Rosie, flicking at a drift of loose hair. 'Situation's plain enough.'

'S'right,' added Megan. 'Sit here all day talkin' when it's doin' yuh gotta get to.'

'Now hold up there — ' began Henry.

'No, you hold up there for once in yuh life, Henry Keyes,' clipped his wife. 'There's a life at stake here and as miserable a way of gettin' to death as you can imagine — or mebbe yuh can't, bein' men! Take it from us, there is.'

'Hell, Rosie, we ain't *that* dumb,' groaned Joe. 'We're as mindful as y'selves to what Esme's facin'.'

'Just look to stayin' that way!'

scowled Megan, comforting the scrambling hands at her skirts.

'T'ain't that easy, though, is it?' said Henry, staring into space again. 'All very well sayin' what's gotta be done, simple enough to know it, but it's one helluva leap from there, to the doin'. Damnit, we ain't no gunfighters. Couldn't stand in the shade of the likes of Larsen's men. When was the last time you handled a gun, Joe? More to the point, when was the last time yuh *fired* one? Bet them old forty-fives of yours ain't seen the light of day since yuh crossed the Utepan.'

'Well,' mumbled Joe, scratching at a sudden irritation in his neck, 'I gotta admit — '

'And you, Frank, when did you last handle a rifle save to raise it against a jack-rabbit?'

'T'ain't a fair question, is it?' spluttered Frank. 'I ain't had the need — '

'Well, yuh got it now!' snapped Nancy, stiffening her arms across her bosom, her eyes flashing. 'Sep Kline, Charlie Bishop, like as not Clyde, and now Esme taken and no tellin' to what end. Enough's enough. End of the line. Can't run now, can we? Can't pack wagons, desert our homes, give up the land, roll away from it all like it was some bad dream. Who's goin' to sleep with that for a nightmare? There ain't one of yuh got the stomach for walkin' outa this if the truth's known. Same goes for m'self, Rosie and Megan — even the young 'uns, them as can think to it — so there ain't no choice, is there? There ain't no more talkin' and debatin' to be done.'

Nancy lowered her arms, walked to the table and stood defiant and formidable at the head of it. 'Womenfolk here'll look to the spreads and the stock. You three know what yuh gotta do.' Her stare moved slowly, piercingly over the faces of the men watching her. 'Best go blow the dust off them guns, hadn't yuh?'

Esme Green seethed quietly, gritted her teeth and worked her hands through a frenzy of brushing and dusting at the skeins of cobwebs tangled in her hair.

She hissed at the threads clinging to her fingers, across the sticky dampness in her neck and back, spat, tossed the hair angrily to her shoulders and eased slowly through the clutter of crates, barrels, trash and junked rubbish in the tight, shadow-filled room at the back of the Trailbender saloon.

She had heard the door thud shut, the key turned to lock it in her scramble as the sidekicks had thrown her across the floor; heard the last of their giggles, the fading footsteps, thud of another door closing, and then only the silence as her eyes had adjusted to the darkness and a shiver passed through her body like the cracking of ice.

It had taken desperate minutes then to adjust her eyes to the stifling gloom, the clutter, to level her breathing, steady the shivering, and for the terror of the ride from the homestead through the silent, moonlit-chilled night to Mission to pass in one last gasp and shudder.

She winced as she struggled between the crates to the barred, dusty window overlooking the alley at the back of the saloon, swallowed on a threatening sob as she peered into the empty shadows, brushed at a trickling tear, turned and slid slowly to the floor.

'What the hell!' she murmured, her mind twisting again on the images of the sidekicks' faces, their mauling hands reaching to rope her to a mount, their mocking sneers, eager, staring eyes.

And the nightmare had not yet begun, she thought, stiffening and then shivering again at the steps approaching the locked door. But it would, it surely would . . .

At the grate of the key being turned.

11

Henry Keyes was suffering a bout of grave misgivings — 'grave', he thought, being the word best fitting from where he was sitting, even though the sun was high and warm in a near cloudless sky, the land empty, silent and peaceful.

Might *look* that way, but give it a nudge on that trail out there into Mission, and you might find other. A whole hornets' nest of 'other', he grunted softly to himself as he eased to the shift of his horse and flicked his gaze to Joe and Frank mounted alongside him.

'This it, then?' said Joe. 'We all agreed?'

Frank ran a warm, wet hand over his weathered face and cleared his throat nervously. 'Spittin' on the wind some, ain't we? One helluva gamble no matter which way yuh look at it.'

'Ain't goin' to be no other than a gamble from any angle, but sittin' weighing the odds ain't helpin'. Stacked all Larsen's way, anyhow, but we gotta try.'

'Yeah, I guess so,' drawled Henry, twisting the loose reins through his fingers. 'Like the women say, wouldn't sleep easy if we didn't. I just wish — '

'Wish all yuh want, we ain't got no fairy godmother lookin' to us,' clipped Joe, his gaze sharpening, then narrowing on the sun-drenched land. 'We do like we've planned: split up and make our separate ways into town, keepin' low, outa sight, unmarked. Not easy, but we can do it if we stay watchful and alert. First thing then is to fix where they're holdin' Esme. Nothin' more. No goin' it alone, no heroics. We meet up soon as we can at them tumble-downs back of the sheriff's office, hole-up 'til sundown, reckon on what we discovered and move again. Simple aim: to get Esme outa town — alive.'

'And then?' asked Frank.

'We figure that when we get to it. Just concentrate for now on Esme.'

'What if — ?' began Henry.

'There's a whole sight more 'what ifs' than we got pesterin' flies!'

'We get in and outa there in one piece, it'll be a miracle,' croaked Henry, his eyes glazing to a flat stare.

'Yeah, well . . . miracles do happen,' quipped Joe. 'Not that I personally ever seen one. First time for everythin', though, ain't there? So let's go see how lucky we can get!'

The three men reined to the trail, broke to a steady gallop and rode easy and in line for a quarter-mile. Not till they reached the sprawl of a ridge above the gently sloping drift to the distant town did they break the pace, exchange glances or another word. There was nothing more to be said, nothing more to be read in the next man's eyes that was not a mirror of what each of them already felt.

Now, at Joe's raised arm as the signal to split, there were quick waves, half murmured grunts, and then only whatever the rest of that day had to offer. Or take.

* * *

At about the same time as the three homesteaders were splitting from the main trail into Mission, Ship O'Toole was drawing heavily on his fourth cigar of the day, squinting against the billowing smoke and pacing endlessly, irritably from window to door, door to window, in his private room above the bar of the Trailbender saloon.

Things, all manner of them, all shapes and sizes, were not going quite as planned. Larsen was over reaching himself, pushing his authority — his menace more like — beyond the bounds of staying smart.

His hands were getting dirty, and this latest move, snatching Clyde Green's wife, bringing her here to the Trailbender, was a whole mile too far. Townfolk only had to hear a whisper of that, and there was no saying how they might react, in spite of their fear. Esme Green was well liked, her man respected.

And there was no saying either what them sodbusters might get to doing.

Then there were Larsen's men; getting too certain, too greedy, too ready to help themselves — and a sight too quick to retaliate when crossed. Carry on like this, and the Trailbender profits would be feeling the pinch.

So, he was debating, smoke seeping through his clenched teeth as he reached the window once again, what to do? What should be his next move?

No edge to be had in talking sense to Larsen. Fellow would simply stare him out with those haunting eyes of his, or worse, get to reckoning on Ship O'Toole having served his useful purpose. No measure of gratitude where Larsen was concerned. No measure of anything, come to it, leastways not of the human kind.

But there was Doc McLean.

Doc had never been for buckling to Larsen. Nothing like. Doc had been for looking to his patients, every man, woman and youngster in town, doing what he saw as his duty by them, and Larsen and his sidekicks could 'go to Hell — which I have no doubt they surely will, come the day, come the man.'

Well, this might be the day for getting a start, letting Doc know he was not alone in his thinking. And, more to the point — right to the very tip of the point, in fact — of finding out for certain if they had their man.

Could be they had. Could be he was here right now, somewhere in town or close by, just waiting on his chance to put on another show of the likes of the Boot Hill shooting at the funeral of Charlie Bishop.

Some shooting; one hell of a gun . . .

That would be it, then, O'Toole decided, stubbing out the half-finished cigar, go see Doc McLean, talk to him, hear what he had to say, see if he had any notion about how they were going to handle things before they got to nightmare.

Or maybe they already had, he thought, swinging from the window as the door crashed open and the least sour-smelling of Larsen's sidekicks tumbled Esme Green into the room and heeled the door closed behind him with a shuddering thud.

'Out!' mouthed the man with a flick of his head, jerk of his thumb, one hand sliding to the leather of his holstered Colt, his gaze tight on the astonished face of Ship O'Toole. 'Mr Larsen don't want the lady holed up in some dirt storeroom. She moves in here. You move out.'

'Now hold on there,' spluttered O'Toole, taking a step forward. 'Yuh can't do that. The hell yuh can't! This is my room, my saloon — I own the place, damn it!'

'Out,' mouthed the man again, idling his weight to one hip. 'Don't let's make this messy. Lady wants some peace and quiet.'

'I don't give a cuss what she wants!' flared O'Toole. 'I'm tellin' yuh — ' He swallowed on his outburst, his stare following Esme as she backed, shuddering and wide-eyed to the wall, her hands working feverishly at her neck, the dirt on her face running to wet streaks under a lathering of cold sweat. 'What yuh done to her, f'Cris'sake?' he croaked, swallowing again. 'If yuh've — '

'I said out, mister, and I mean out.' The man tapped a stiffening finger over the holster. 'You just go get one of yuh gals to give the lady a hand here. Water for washin' and a clean dress. Larsen's orders. So just do it, eh?'

O'Toole trembled on the brink of another outburst, dragged his stare from Esme, gazed at the man and came slowly to the door as it swung open under the sidekick's hand.

'I just hope yuh know — ' he began, but was promptly pushed to the corridor beyond the room, pushed again as the man closed and locked the door behind him and bundled him on to the head of the stairs above the saloon.

'Keep yuh nose clean and outa things if yuh know what's good for yuh,' drawled the man, a grin sliding over his dirt-grained lips. 'Go get that gal — now, before Larsen figures yuh for draggin' yuh heels. He don't stand too well to heel-draggin'.'

O'Toole mouthed a silent curse and passed quickly down the stairs to the group of bar girls lounging at the gaming tables.

Get this done and then get to Doc McLean, he resolved, gesturing to the nearest of the girls. The nightmare was here.

* * *

Esme waited, tight to the wall, the shudders through her body easing to spasms of chill shivers, and did not move till the last of the footsteps had faded from the corridor and the silence settled again like the stillness after a storm.

Her gaze shifted quickly over the room, to the neatly covered bed, the side table, chairs, mirrors, paintings on the walls, richly coloured square of expensive carpet, the wardrobe, a second table scattered with O'Toole's belongings — timepiece, loose coinage, bottle of scented water, cravat, cufflinks — and slowly, carefully to the single window where the heavy velvet drapes stood open to the street below.

She waited another minute, licked her lips, tossed the straggle of hanging hair to her neck, and crossed softly, as stealthily as a stalking cat, to the glare of sunlight.

She was a while then before moving closer to take in the line of buildings opposite: Cartwright's store, the saddlery, meat vendor, Jonas Whitman's barbering and shaving shop, long-time closed and abandoned sheds and the tumble of buildings behind them, drift of smoke from the livery far end of the street, the hitching rails, boardwalks, scattering of folk going silently, hurriedly about their business, stretches of brightness, stiff, sentinel shadows.

And there, in the deepest of them, his gaze fixed on the saloon window, a nod and slanted grin of recognition greeting her as she edged closer to the pane, the sidekick who had dragged her from the storeroom.

'Sonofabitch!' she muttered, as she watched the man push himself clear of a post and harden his gaze on the window. Next time he laid a mauling hand on her . . .

The man had stepped from the shadow to the edge of the boardwalk, hands planted on his hips, his eyes sharp as pinpricks of light in a long tunnel, his tongue licking over his lips, when the shot shattered the silence and stillness as if the day had been ripped apart savagely, brutally and crunched to a ball.

Esme gasped, shivered and was falling back from the window as the sidekick's body spun where it stood, seemed for endless moments to hang like a crumpling mound of rags, a bloodstain spreading fast and deep, before thudding to the dirt and raising a cloud of drifting dust.

The echo of the single, thundering blaze hung in the street like a haunting that gripped and was here to stay.

12

Sheriff Tamms's shaking hand had been hovering over the half-empty bottle of whiskey when the roar and blaze of the shot had jerked him from his misty-eyed reach and sent the bottle crashing to the floor of the dark, shadowed room at the back of his office.

Now, with the echo of the blast spinning somewhere in the liquored depths of his fuddled head, he could only stare at the shattered glass, the seeping, widening pool of liquid and moan softly to himself in his rocking perch on the end of the unmade bed.

Time was when he would have been into the street, a Winchester tight in his grip, faster than a fly from flame. Time was when he would have been in control, barking his orders, ranging his deputies and pinning down the shootist fool enough to disturb the peace of his town before the fellow had drawn breath.

Time was when he might have had good cause to gun the sonofabitch right where he stood; one shot, clean and true, no messing. Time was . . . What the hell! All that had been way back, long before Larsen and his sidekicks.

Only priority right now was to go check he had another bottle in the cupboard there.

Abe Cartwright had been tidying the shelves of his store when the shot had ripped into the silence like a blade slitting broadcloth.

He had fallen back from the rickety steps, lost his footing, then his balance, stumbled across a stacked heap of besoms and axe handles, slithered into an opened sack of beans, scattering the contents thick and far, reached to support himself against the counter, sent three candy jars flying, staggered on to upset a pile of blankets, and finally come to rest on his knees in the doorway to the boardwalk.

124

He had blinked tight and fast on the sight of the body sprawled in the street and been the only man close enough, he reckoned, to see the fellow's last twitch behind his final groan.

Smoke had billowed in a sudden, clamouring cloud of sparks and ash at the livery; Jonas Whitman had cut his thumb sharpening a razor; a dozing drunk in the shadows at the rear of the saloon had figured the shot for a clap of thunder and scurried for cover against imagined rain; a bar girl had screamed, another slid from the lap of a sidekick at his thrusting jump to his feet as he sprang to join the surge of Larsen's men to the batwings; Ship O'Toole had swallowed and sweated; the drinkers froze where they stood, no longer drinking.

Only Doc McLean, his hat set neatly on his head, drape of his frock coat failing tidily to his newly pressed pants, had gone about his day with his usual calm, closing the door to his surgery quietly, taking a firm hold on his medicine bag and stepping with an air of resigned duty to the street in the direction of the dead body.

And wondering too how long it would be before Larsen put in a cold-eyed appearance.

★ ★ ★

Joe Medley, Henry Keyes and Frank Cooper — by now well into the stealth of their separate approaches to the outskirts of town — had reined up at the roar and echo of the shot, frowns creasing their soaked brows, dismounted and dived for the nearest cover.

Joe had spat the dirt from his mouth and snuggled deeper into the shade of an outcrop. No saying why the shot had been fired, he thought. No saying for certain whose finger on the trigger, but there was no doubting the sound: the same as he had heard that morning on Boot Hill the day they had buried Charlie. Fast Colt, custom-built for one man's hands. No mistaking it. Still hear the echo, almost feel the blaze. Hell, so just who, just what . . . ?

But Joe had simply wiped his face and waited. Time would come soon enough when he had some answers.

Henry had scrambled into the cover of rough brush and collapsed in a sprawl of already aching limbs and heavy breathing. He too had recognized the sound of the shot, and taken no comfort in the roar of it. Damn it, just what was going on there in town; just what were they about to sneak their way into; what would they find, *who* would they find, and would they stay alive long enough to come even close to answers?

But, like Joe, Henry had simply waited, chillingly conscious that rough brush was no guard against spitting lead.

Frank had stayed flat and as near lifeless as he could make himself in the dirt of open land. His thoughts, crackling like burning firewood through his mind, had concentrated almost entirely on Esme.

Hell, if it was possible the gunfighter they had hauled half-dead out of the 'Pan had somehow survived, he was about the last person to go shooting Esme, not in cold blood, not for the hell of it, not unless she was too far gone to . . . That was fool thinkin'!

So maybe that raging Colt had been turned on Larsen. Maybe there had been a showdown. One shot? Only one way to find out.

But it was almost a half-hour before the three homesteaders had summoned the courage to scramble back to their mounts and head ever closer to the waiting town. Thought common to each of them at that time was the need to go easy, stay calm, stay level-headed.

No man hurried into Hell, did he?

★   ★   ★

Esme Green had taken almost that same half-hour before daring to edge back to the window.

She had heard the raised voices, startled shouts, stifled screams in the bar below her; heard the thudding of boots to boardwalks, the curses, the sudden, hollow silence. There had been the snort of a horse, the sound of a child crying, clang of a dropped pail, the sizzling, sneezing hiss of steam at the forge, and then, from the dark depths of the corridor the other side of the door, the tread of measured steps, pausing, moving on, no hurry, no quickening of the pace, not even when they reached the head of the stairs and descended slowly, casually to the bar. No voices then. Nothing.

Esme had swallowed, gritted her teeth and moved back to the window.

It had been only minutes before Larsen stepped from the boardwalk to the sunlit street, a black drifting shape that cast its shadow like a long claw-hooked limb, stepping soundlessly between the small group gathered at the body, dismissive of comments and gestures, its gaze fixed and tight.

The man glanced quickly at Doc McLean, stared at the body, touched it with the tip of his boot, raised his head and let the strange coloured eyes slip carefully along the line of buildings, the gaze settling on windows, rooftops, the stiff fingers of pipe chimneys.

The suddenness of the man's reach for his holstered Colt made Esme blink, catch her breath, and then shudder at the bite of the shot that spat lead into Abe Cartwright's left arm.

Larsen's lips twitched on a soft grin as he watched the storekeeper reel back, blood bubbling through his fingers clutching the wound, but he made no sound, said nothing as he turned, glanced at Esme and made his way back to the saloon, retracing almost exactly the steps he had taken only minutes before.

Nobody in the street moved, made a sound, until Doc McLean led Abe

Cartwright into the shade of his littered store.

All that was left then to that day was the body and the pestering flies as two men dragged the mess out of sight.

13

'Best I can do,' grunted Doc McLean, checking over the bandaging on Abe Cartwright's arm. 'Be a mite stiff for a while, but yuh'll live. Lucky for you Larsen was in a generous mood!'

'Hell,' winced Abe, 'what the sonofabitch have to go do that for? I ain't got no argument with the fella. Had the run of the store for long enough *and* he ain't paid a bean!'

'Spite, retribution, amounts to the same thing,' said Doc, closing his medicine bag with a decisive click. 'Somebody had to pay for what happened out there. Yuh just happened to be nearest.'

Abe winced again as he stretched the bandaged arm. 'But that's it, ain't it?' he said, his stare black and hollow in his pallid face. 'What *did* happen out there? Who shot that scumbag? Where was the fella holed-up, f'Cris'sake? No place I could figure. But he must have been close. Had to be. And did yuh hear that shot, the roar of it, that damned echo? I ain't never heard a shot like that before.' Abe's black stare flashed on the whites of his eyes. 'Where's the fella now? Answer me that.'

'Can't,' said Doc, resting a hand on his bag. 'Can't, 'cus I don't know. Mebbe he's here in town somewhere.'

'Where, in God's name? Yuh tell me where a fella the likes of what he must be could hide himself in a squat like Mission? Ain't no place, none I can think of, not unless he's got the happy knack of turnin' himself into a tick or a termite; gets himself buried 'tween blankets or 'neath floorboards! Come on, Doc, t'ain't possible, is it? And who's goin' to give shelter to some gunfightin' stranger when there's vermin the cut of Larsen about who don't give a cuss who he riddles his lead through?'

'So mebbe the fella operates outa

133

town,' shrugged Doc. 'Rides in when he's comin' about his business.'

'Oh,' frowned Abe, 'and just what sorta business would that be? You got some notion on it?' He eased the bandaged arm to his side and narrowed his gaze on Doc McLean's carefully vacant stare into the sunlit street. 'I known yuh for a long whiles, Doc. Read yuh like a book. What yuh sayin' here?'

'The shootin' out at Charlie Bishop's funeral, what happened out there today, all one and the same, aren't they?' murmured Doc. 'All aimed at Larsen, weakenin' him, 'til mebbe he'll be left standin' alone.'

'Somebody with a grudge against Larsen festerin' fit to burst? That what yuh sayin'?'

Doc sighed and tapped his fingers over his bag. 'Mebbe. Somethin' like that.'

'And them homesteadin' folk, and Esme Green held out there like she is, they figure in this?'

Doc turned his stare from the

window to Abe's sweat-smeared face. 'Could be they do at that.' His fingers gripped the handle of the bag until the knuckles whitened. 'Tell yuh somethin', though,' he added in a voice that had sunk to a croak, 'whoever this fella is, wherever he is, for whatever reason he's here, he ain't done yet. Not by a long shot, he ain't.'

The pain in Abe Cartwright's arm had numbed to a dull throb.

*   *   *

Ship O'Toole had slipped, slithered, sidled and slunk his way into the darkest corner of the bar, his back to the wall, an unlit cigar tight between his teeth, his face flushed, eyes like a hawk's on the smoke-hazed, shadowed light.

Just watch that group of Larsen's men there, he was thinking, his fingers working nervously at the mother-of-pearl buttons on his waistcoat. No saying where Larsen's muttered orders to them might be leading. All the way to Hell and back judging by the mean glints in their eyes, the sidelong glances between scowls, fidgeting hands never more than a fast finger from holstered Colts. And much more of that cheap whiskey down their throats . . .

He swallowed on a suddenly gripping, sweat-stained collar. Damn it, another bottle of that and this place might be looking more like a bad meat slaughterhouse than a saloon bar. Even the girls pouting there had lost their appeal.

He gulped, shifting his gaze to the stairs, the dark spread of the corridor at the head of them, the doors to the rooms . . . Esme Green behind one of them.

He wondered if the girl he had sent to look to her was still there, dragging out the washing and dressing for as long as she could, before Larsen's curiosity, impatience, whatever it was seeped through that warped body of his, lay behind the multi-coloured eyes, got the better of him and he took a stroll from the room not two doors from where the woman was held. Worse, had her dragged to him.

Or maybe Larsen had other thoughts on his mind ... thoughts of another sidekick gunned to the dirt ... thoughts of how he might get to the fellow responsible, what he would do if a search proved fruitless.

No hand hereabouts going to be raised against him, whatever he decided, not a man with guts to do more than stand in the nearest, deepest shadow, watch and wait.

Except perhaps for Doc McLean.

Give it a while longer, he mused, maybe till a hint of sundown, and he would go see him, just as he had planned, talk to him, get to figuring on what to do.

Hold it, what was that barbering fellow, Jonas Whitman, hovering at the batwings like some wide-eyed kid for? Why was he pushing them open, stepping to the bar — he only ever drank on Fridays — and why, damn it, was he heading this way, his face as white and drawn as the ghost he might have seen?

'We got big trouble brewin',' he whispered, sidling to O'Toole's side. 'Real big. Know what, them sodbusters are in town. Seen one of them back of my place. There's another skulkin' round the sheriff's office. And old Spinhead, drunk as he is, reckons he spotted one an hour back, far end of town.'

The barber's eyes bulged. 'So what we goin' to do? Larsen spots 'em here there'll be a bloodbath!'

★ ★ ★

'Sorry, losin' my grip here,' shuddered the girl as the brush snagged for a second in its stroke through Esme's tumbling waves of hair. 'Give a whole lot to be doin' anythin' but this.' She shuddered again and stood back. 'Just ain't human.'

'Don't worry,' said Esme, turning to face the girl. 'Do the same m'self in your place. No choice, have yuh?' She laid a reassuring hand on the girl's arm, smiled softly, then spun the folds of the dress to a swirling dance, adjusted the drape of the collar and stared at herself in the mirror. 'Wouldn't be my choice. Don't like the colour, but . . . How do I look?'

The girl gulped and bit nervously on her bottom lip. 'Hell, lady, I just don't know how yuh can be so calm about all this. If it were me standin' where you are — '

'Ah,' said Esme, turning again, her gaze suddenly colder and sharper, 'but that's the point, that's what I wanna hear. No disrespect, but yuh have been right where I am. Yuh know what it's all about with them scum down there. Probably more than most. So tell me. Everythin'.'

'Hell,' sighed the girl, her shoulders slumping, 'take the best part of a week to do that! But I figure yuh thinkin'.

This ain't exactly an everyday situation for yuh, is it? Yuh wouldn't know, bein' who yuh are, life yuh been leadin' — and no disrespect there neither. Just wish I'd had half the chance.'

The girl threw the brush to the bed, crossed the room to the window and stared into the street for a long, thoughtful moment. 'Weren't so bad here for me and the girls 'til Larsen and his men rode in,' she began. 'Just bar girl life, no better, no worse than it ever gets. O'Toole ain't the best, but I seen his type a whole sight meaner. But Larsen, he's somethin' else.'

She paused, stiffening, the stare glazed and unblinking. 'Know all about yuh, lady, where yuh from, what yuh been goin' through out there on yuh spread; you and yuh neighbours along of yuh. Ain't a deal the girls don't get to hear, one way or another. Know why yuh've been brought in like yuh have. Why they're havin' yuh tarted up like this. Yuh standin' hostage, lady, against Larsen gettin' what he wants. And he

140

will. He always does. I got the scars to prove it.'

The girl turned slowly from the window, her young, bright-eyed face drawn to a grey mask. 'Truth of it — I wouldn't give two-bits for yuh future from here on. I seen women dead at Larsen's hands inside a coupla days. They all died wishin' it'd come sooner.'

Esme swallowed and squirmed against a chilled sweat on her back.

'Only thing bein',' the girl went on, crossing the room to the small table, ''t'ain't all goin' quite Larsen's way right now. He figures on there bein' a gunfighter on the loose, here or close by. Some reckon as how he knows the fella from way back.' She shrugged. 'No saying, not yet, but the town's sure as hell getting spooked some. Wouldn't take more than . . . ' She shrugged again. 'Wishful thinkin'.'

'Has there been any talk about — ?' began Esme, croakily.

'Yuh husband? That what yuh askin'? Can't say specific. All I can tell yuh is that Larsen sent a coupla fellas out to the trail into Carver. They ain't back yet.'

The chilled sweat seemed to seep through to Esme's bones.

'Look,' said the girl, lifting the folds of her skirts to remove a pair of scissors from the grip of her garter, 'this is the best I can do for yuh. Ain't much of a weapon, but if yuh snuggle 'em tight in that garter I've given yuh, who knows, yuh might get lucky. Sorry it ain't more.'

'Thanks,' said Esme, taking the scissors in a shaking hand.

The girl smiled softly, let her touch settle gently, briefly on Esme's shoulder, then crossed to the door. 'Time I wasn't here,' she murmured. 'Don't worry, me and the girls'll be lookin' to yuh. Do the best we can.' She winked, paused, one hand on the knob, and added, 'By the way, yuh right, that colour don't suit yuh!'

Esme was a while before she moved from that spot in the shadowed room, her limbs numb, body cold, her thoughts spinning helplessly through a mayhem of images, the silence closing in as if to drown her.

When she did move, with a sudden sigh, shudder, toss of the hair across her shoulders, it was to hide the scissors in a place befitting the finest traditions of bar-girl strategy.

14

Do not spit; do not shift a boot, a leg, a hand, and if you really do have a need to blink, then do it real soft, like a moth on the night, and only once if you still want to be here to see the light come up again.

Frank Cooper risked the blink, fast and fitful, breathed deeply and winced softly at the ache in his limbs. Ten minutes of tight, tensed squatting was one thing, a whole hour of it another matter. But, even so, he was here, in town, his mount hitched away safe as he could find, and himself — dare he think it? — as undetected as a grain of dirt in a desert. Or so it seemed from here, buried in the jumble back of the livery.

All the cover he needed, any amount of thick, hugging shadows, and not that much longer, he reckoned, to the sun up there burning itself out for the day and slipping far side of the horizon. Time then to move again, figure on getting teamed up with Joe. Last he had seen of him he had been scurrying like a cat close to the sheriff's office.

But what, he wondered, of Henry? No sign of him, not a flicker.

He blinked again, swallowed, and eased the merest fraction higher for a broader view of the livery. Familiar twist of smoke, tired snorts of the few stabled horses, buzz of flies, crow there rummaging in the scattered straw, nothing of Billhook, the blacksmith. Sleeping off the afternoon heat, resting up with a welcome drink, or maybe still lingering somewhere in town, picking up whatever news there was of that single gunshot, listening to the rumours?

Wondering more like what Larsen was planning next.

Frank settled back, his thoughts spinning on the state of Esme, Clyde's progress towards Carver City — reckoning for him to be well within sight of

Cloud Top, taking the higher route for speed if he had any sense — or had the ride not gone quite as planned? Supposing Larsen had figured . . .

Forget it, he thought. Rambling like that got him nowhere. Had all he needed for one mind to handle all around him.

Quiet enough now, he reckoned, and the livery deserted. He glanced towards the empty street, the shadows back of its line of buildings. They would be the place to be next, he decided; an almost straight run through to the sheriff's office. Stay silent, stay low and he could be teaming up with Joe within the hour.

Two minutes later, Frank Cooper had risen from his cover at the livery and stared directly into the depths of the barrel of a Colt levelled precisely at the centre of his forehead.

'Yuh all rested up there, fella?' drawled the voice behind it. 'Been a while waitin' on yuh!'

Joe Medley's luck had run out at the fall of his first untidy step.

He had reached the rear of Sheriff Tamms's office with ease, in silence and with barely the slip of his own shadow to mark his progress. No problem, he had thought through a soft, satisfied smile. Homesteading was maybe no ground training for playing out the role of skulking gunman, but he had taken to it naturally enough. Seemed to have a natural flair. Sometimes a fellow was a while getting to realize his hidden potential.

Next move, he had reckoned, resting in the shade of the alley between the office and a deserted storehouse, was to get to that liquor-sodden sheriff sweating it out in there in the dregs of cheap whiskey, sober him up sufficient to get his mouth working on what he knew of Esme and Larsen's planning, then wait for Frank holed up at the livery to join him.

Henry was another matter. Just where in hell had he managed to bury himself?

Joe had taken a firmer grip on the Colt weighing heavy in his hand, licked his lips, and eased forward, steps as light as a feather across the dirt, taking care to keep his boots clear of anything that might move, creak or make a sound of any sort. Sheriff Tamms might be liquor-fuddled, but even a drunk could get to being jumpy if he suspected a trespasser across his private patch.

But it might have served Joe a whole lot better if he had pondered on how a drunken lawman disposed of his empty bottles. He was to find out in the step that brought him to the corner of the office; a step that crunched over dirt and the slivers of broken glass beneath it.

The crack split the silence like a gunshot.

Joe's limbs were suddenly leaden, the right boot flat on the glass as he winced, screwed his eyes, sweat breaking bright and beaded on his brow, and stayed rooted to the spot. He could have been in luck with Sheriff Tamms locked in his whiskey haze and this end of the town seemingly deserted, but he had not reckoned on the chance wandering of one of Larsen's sidekicks scouring the area for a clue to the whereabouts of the mystery shootist.

Not reckoned either on the man's instant reaction, the swift dart to the source of the crack, a Winchester already primed and levelled straight as a shaft of light at Joe's gut.

'A sodbuster!' the man had leered. 'Well, now, ain't you just one for strayin' some. Lost yuh way, mister'? Yuh found one helluva place to fetch up!' The leer had faded, the scarred, weathered face darkened, but the rifle stayed steady. 'Drop the piece, fella. Yuh done all yuh strayin' for one day.'

★ ★ ★

Henry Keyes, meantime, had lost his way and a deal of his nerve with it.

He was shivering in spite of the still balmy heat of the afternoon, his fingers twitching endlessly from a holstered gun to the buttons on his shirt, to the gritty darkness of his stubble, his lips, the corners of his squinting eyes.

How he had got to where he was — somewhere close to the back-room door of the Trailbender — he had no clear notion, only that he had, and now had no idea of where to go next or precisely what to do.

This was not for him, he had decided, on a long, parched, pinching swallow that seemed to claw a path to the pit of his stomach. Hell, he would stand to do his best by Esme along with any man, but when it came to the figuring of it, holstering a Colt, putting his life right there on the line, he was no better than the ring-tail he had back there on the spread.

Nothing to be proud of neither. Hard to look Clyde Green in the eye and admit to it. And you could bet Joe Medley would have some barbed comment minute he showed up — if he ever did — not to mention Frank who was never one to choose his words.

There might, of course, be something he could do. He could pull himself together, get a grip, clear his thinking and try opening that door there. A gnawing instinct was telling him that if Esme was being held hostage, it would be somewhere in the saloon, where Larsen and his men could keep a close eye on her.

So maybe, if he could summon the courage, he could sneak in; just get to listening, watching, noting; figure the lie of the land, where the scum were holding Esme, and then, when the time came . . .

Henry Keyes' other weakness of resolve was his haste, at the first surge of a notion, to get to it, get it done while the nerve held.

And so it was, seconds later, he was moving to the back-room door of the

Trailbender without a thought for what he might be facing, or worse, just who might be watching from the window, intent only on the door, the hope it had not been locked and would open to the softest touch.

It did — with Henry still three steps short of it and staring glassy-eyed and sweat-blurred into the looming bulk of a sidekick, his smile like a tooth-filled fissure across his face, his gun already blazing from his hand to bury a stream of lead into Henry's left arm.

'Careless,' was all the man drawled, shaking his head.

★   ★   ★

By five o'clock that evening, with the light fading, the sun setting, the flies seeking night shelter, the town of Mission lay in a deep slumber of silence. No one strayed to the empty main street, no one watched from the darkening windows, risked the shadows or dared their luck on an evening stroll.

And most, given the events of the day, were all for seeing the darkness creep in and the moon to hide.

But that did not include Larsen and his sidekicks gathered in the smoke-smeared bar of the saloon. They, as they had so often reminded the good folk of Mission, were night birds, at their most decisive through the hours of the owl.

And this night had not yet begun.

15

Ship O'Toole had put the gathering night to his own advantage and made his getaway from the saloon bar — on the excuse of attending to some 'business' with Jonas Whitman across the street — a while before Larsen had joined his men.

Now, standing in the deepest of the shadows beyond the soft glow of the lantern light in Doc McLean's back parlour, he was listening to the sound of his own voice like a man in a trance.

'Sonofabitch is holdin' Esme Green in my room — *my* room, would yuh believe? Tarted her up like somethin' out of a cat house . . . and yuh don't have to ask for why! God knows what sorta state she'll be in come mornin', if she gets that far.

'And them hare-brained, sodbustin' neighbours of hers ain't helped none, sneakin' into town like that, might've known they wouldn't get more than a handful of steps before Larsen's men picked 'em up. They ain't cut out for standin' to gunfighters. Mean well, o'course, but, hell, they've as good as handed Larsen a winnin' hand.'

He paused, fumbling through his jacket pockets for his cigar case. 'Got Joe Medley, Henry Keyes — he's bleedin' some — and Frank Cooper locked and under guard in my store-room. Hell, Doc, place is like a State Penitentiary! What's Larsen figurin' on doin' with all these bodies — or mebbe they're just that: bodies. Dead bodies!'

He paused again, flicking a cigar through his fingers. 'What we goin' to do, Doc? Gotta do somethin', f'Cris'sake. Can't just sit back waitin' on that mystery gunfighter gettin' to work again. Hell, he might not even be here. Chances are he's gone, ridden out. Even he ain't fool enough to stand against odds the likes of the sort Larsen's stackin' up.'

'Yuh goin' to light that thing, offer me one, or save it for another time?' said Doc, nodding at the unlit cigar in O'Toole's fingers.

'What? Oh, sure, help y'self.'

They lit the cigars, drew on them and blew the smoke thoughtfully through the lantern light.

'Know what I reckon, Doc?' O'Toole continued. 'I reckon for them sod-busters doin' a deal with Larsen: their lives and freedom, Esme along of 'em, for leavin' their spreads to the railroad. Be a way out for 'em, wouldn't it? Got everythin' to lose if they don't.'

'And yuh figure for Larsen goin' along with that?' asked Doc.

'Settles the issue for him: he gets what he came for, railroad stays happy, sodbusters move on, just grateful to be alive. Them farmin' fellas are family folk. Ain't no risk worth takin' that threatens their women and young 'uns.'

'Them 'farming' fellas as yuh put it don't include Clyde Green right now, do they?' said Doc carefully from behind a cloud of curling smoke, his gaze narrowed. 'He ain't bein' held in yuh storeroom.'

O'Toole studied the glowing tip of his cigar. 'Yeah, well,' he murmured, 'that seems like another story, don't it? If Green was fool enough to figure on makin' it to Carver City — *and* leave that pretty wife of his alone on his spread — hell, he was askin' for trouble. Larsen would've reckoned on somethin' like that.' He lifted his eye slowly from the cigar. 'He sent a couple of his boys out to the trail . . . and that's somethin' else we don't have to ask for why. I doubt if Green made it outa the Utepan.'

Doc grunted and stepped to the parlour-room window overlooking the street where the light now had faded to no more than soft skimmings through the thickening shadows. 'And we stood back all these months and let it happen,' he said, his back to O'Toole, the cigar smoke trailing like grey breath to the panes. 'Just gave Larsen a free hand, didn't we? Too scared, too cowardly to raise so much as a whisper of protest, while good men died and more are goin' to follow.'

'But what if that gunfighter fella we ain't yet set eyes on — ' began O'Toole, but fell silent at Doc's raised arm. 'What yuh seen? Somethin' happenin' out there?' he hissed, coming to Doc's side.

'Judgin' by the way them scumbags of Larsen's are gatherin' there front of your saloon, I'd say there's goin' to be a whole heap of somethin' happenin'!'

The smoke from O'Toole's cigar had curled into his eyes as he leaned forward to squint into the street. 'In God's name, what now?' he croaked, his gaze watering on the blurred dazzle of lantern light and the shapes of the figures gathering like moths behind it.

Only Doc McLean shifted his concentration at the creak of a floorboard in the room above the silent, smoke-hazed parlour.

* * *

They strolled, lounged, sidled and idled their way through the batwings to the boardwalk; a dozen scruffily dressed, unwashed, black-stubbled men, Colts slung easy to the draw, hands loose, fingers flexing to the mocking authority behind their sneers and leers, the ice-cold flatness in their stares.

Slowly, with the arrogance of a rabble of mutinous troopers, they shambled into line, silent now save for the hawking spits, crease of leather where the leanest of them rocked impatiently on his heels, until a tall, stony-faced man with a skin as cracked and pitted as a dry-bed creek stream, stepped forward, drew his Colt and fired two shots high into the balmy night air.

'Get yuh out here, every last one,' he shouted above the fading echo of the shots. 'Yuh hear me? Men, women, brats, anythin' walkin' and breathin' in this godforsaken dump.'

Lanterns flickered into life at windows; doors creaked and scraped open; voices murmured fearfully; shapes grew in shadows; faces sweated, eyes gleamed, watchful and uncertain.

'Move! Now!' shouted the man again.

Abe Cartwright soothed his good hand over the wounded arm in its sling and shuffled to the boardwalk fronting his store. Jones Whitman dried his hands on a towel, flicked the blade of the cut-throat razor to its sheath, pocketed it and eased carefully to the edge of the straggle of townfolk gathering in the street.

Billhook, the blacksmith, reached instinctively for a hammer and loomed out of the haze of his forge like a cloud. Sheriff Tamms staggered into the night, blinked as if bewildered by the sudden space, spun through a circle, rolled, set his feet apart for his balance and gulped on the half-empty bottle tight in his grip.

'What the hell's goin' on?' croaked

O'Toole, the cigar in his fingers still glowing as he tumbled from Doc McLean's front parlour and glared at the line of men ranged across the front of the Trailbender.

'Hold it,' said Doc, a restraining hand on the saloon-keeper's arm as he came to his side. 'Them fellas ain't for messin' with, not in that mood they ain't. Hear 'em out.'

Slowly, silently the street filled with townfolk, some whispering nervously to neighbours, some slipping a protective arm to the shoulders of the women; mothers herding young ones to their skirts, bolder-faced youths hitching thumbs in belts and braces; a drunk staring from the shadows and vowing never to touch another drop. All with their gazes fixed then on the line of Larsen's men, the stony-faced spokesman idling the Colt loosely at his hip.

'Right, yuh all here? Nobody missin'? Better not be,' he drawled, easing his weight to one leg. 'Ain't for sayin' this more than once, so yuh'd best listen up real good.' His eyes flicked over the waiting, frowning, twitching faces. 'Mr Larsen ain't happy, not one bit happy, and we ain't for havin' that, are we?' Nobody moved, nobody murmured. ''Course we ain't, 'cus we all know where that might lead. Seen it before, ain't we? So we're goin' to have to do somethin' about it — and fast.'

The man spun the Colt through his fingers. 'We got somebody here in town who's gotten himself a whole lot too frisky with some fancy Colt he's totin'. Figures himself for bein' real smart. Well, let me tell yuh somethin', his luck's just run out, every last drop of it. Mr Larsen ain't for havin' him about no more. Now, unless there's any one of yuh here who happens to know where this scumbag might be holed-up, who ain't had the stomach this far to speak his mind, me and the boys are goin' to get busy. Anybody got anythin' to say?'

Again, nobody moved, nobody made

a sound, save for the drunk who belched and Ship O'Toole, who coughed on a surge of cigar smoke.

'Suit y'selves. Yuh had yuh chance.' The man spun the Colt to its holster and stiffened to his full, bony height. 'Beginnin' now, we're takin' this town apart, every last stick of it, every place standin', 'til there ain't a corner of it that ain't been searched down to the last speck of dust. And that includes every nook and cranny of yuh homes.' A grin slid cynically over his lips. 'Woe betide anybody hidin' somethin' they shouldn't.'

The man took a slow step to the edge of the boardwalk. 'Yuh understand? I made myself clear? Better had, 'cus we're lookin' here for yuh full co-operation — which means first as lifts a finger against us is a dead man. Woman, come to that. We ain't fussed.' The grin spread to a twisted smile. 'So let's get to it, shall we? Goin' to be a busy night, longer if that's what it takes, 'cus we ain't stoppin' 'til we find this rat.'

The crowd stayed unmoving, still silent, their gazes blank and empty, only the gleaming sweat on their faces mirroring the fears pounding in their heads.

'Folk goin' to stand for this?' hissed O'Toole in Doc's ear.

'They got any choice?' said Doc.

O'Toole gripped the cigar tight between his teeth. 'Hell,' he hissed again. 'Where's that sonofabitch, Larsen, skulkin'?'

'Back in the bar. He won't cross them batwings 'til it's necessary.'

'What's with him? He scared or somethin'?'

'Watchful,' murmured Doc. 'Wouldn't you be in his boots?'

O'Toole removed the cigar. 'Yuh mean . . . ' he began. 'Yuh sayin' as how he's reckonin' — ?'

'I ain't sayin' nothin',' said Doc, his gaze narrowed on the sidekicks and the slowly dispersing townfolk, 'exceptin' as how we should mebbe get a touch busy ourselves.'

'What yuh thinkin'?'

'I'm thinkin', Mr O'Toole, as how them sidekicks are goin' to be a mite preoccupied for a while, and Larsen's put all his hostage eggs in one basket, ain't he? All tight as ticks there in your saloon.'

'Mebbe we could get — '

'Mebbe a lot of things. But right now, yuh get back to yuh business and stay there. I'll do the figurin' from here on.'

'Knew I could rely on yuh, Doc,' grinned O'Toole.

'Yeah, well, we might have the eggs in one basket, but let's not get to countin' chickens. Just warn Billhook there as how I wanna see him.'

O'Toole grunted, heeled the cigar and moved away to thread a path through the gathering to the saloon. Doc turned back to his front door standing open to the soft lantern light in the parlour. Rubbish the place all they liked, he was thinking as he headed indoors, the sidekicks would find nothing here of the slightest interest. Not now. They were going to be too late.

The bird had flown.

16

'What's happenin' out there? Some-thin's happenin'.' Joe Medley stumbled his way through the mound of crates and trash in the storeroom at the back of the Trailbender, reached the window, thrust a hand between the bars and scrubbed at the layers of dust and grime. 'Yuh hear that? Them sidekicks are movin'.' He scrubbed again, hissing on his curses. 'Damn it, hardly see a thing!'

'Wouldn't count to nothin' if yuh could,' groaned Frank Cooper from the dusty shadows. 'We ain't goin' no place, not yet awhile.'

'Hey, give me a hand here, will yuh?' winced Henry Keyes, struggling to adjust the torn shirtsleeve bandage on his arm. 'Hell, I reckon I lost more blood — '

'Hold in there, fella,' said Joe, still

167

scrubbing at the windowpane, 'I gotta notion things are movin'. Mebbe we ain't for bein' holed-up here for much longer.'

'Yeah, and mebbe we are,' groaned Frank again, tightening the bandaging on Henry's arm. 'I just get to thinkin' about the women back there on the spreads. My Megan can get to bein' awful fidgety come sundown.'

'The hell with bein' night-spooked,' snapped Joe. 'We gotta whole heap of fidgetin' to figure right here. Women'll look to themselves, sure enough — when don't they? — so let's just get to concentratin' . . . Hold it!' he shushed, pressing his face to the bars. 'There's somebody out there, slippin' in and out of them shadows like a scroungin' hound. T'ain't no sidekick neither. One of them townfolk.'

'Most of 'em in Larsen's pocket!' muttered Frank.

'Not this one,' murmured Joe. 'Not the way he's movin'. Could be we're gettin' lucky.'

Henry Keyes winced again and wiped a bloodstained hand down his pants. Frank Cooper went back to the dusty shadows by the door and listened for the slightest sound beyond it. Nothing, not so much as the twitch of a cricket.

'Fella's still there,' hissed Joe. 'And he's gettin' closer.'

'Hope he's makin' a better job of it than we did!' quipped Frank.

'Helluva mess we made, and there ain't sayin' other,' added Henry, clearing another smear of blood. 'Get to bleedin' to death here!'

'Will yuh just cut the moanin'?' said Joe, still with his face pressed to the bars.

'Well, mebbe yuh ain't seein' this same as we are,' hissed Frank angrily. 'Mebbe it ain't yet occurred to you, Joe Medley, as how we're right where that sonofabitch Larsen wants us, and I wouldn't give two spits to a tin can for our chances of comin' out of it anythin' like alive. Minute it suits him — '

'We ain't dead yet, are we?' clipped Joe. 'We ain't seen nothin' yet of Larsen neither. Could be he's figurin' on doin' some sorta deal with us. Damn it, he's got Esme here some place; he's got us; he knows we left our families out there on the spreads. Got a full hand, ain't he? Deal it any way he likes.'

Henry shifted uncomfortably and gripped his arm. 'Yuh ever known Larsen do any dealin' save from the bottom of the deck? He ain't goin' to leave us alive, is he? Tell them railroad types any story he wants: say as how we got to doin' all the spoilin', wouldn't see sense, wouldn't negotiate, so it went from heated words to hot lead and his men were only retaliatin' in self-defence. Simple as that.' He groaned and spat noisily. 'Bet yuh sweet life Clyde Green's dead as old stone, and I wouldn't give the dirt on my boot for Esme's future.'

'Yeah, well,' muttered Joe, wiping cobwebs, dust and sweat from his face, 'I gotta admit as how it don't look that good. Did our best, but mebbe we did over-reach ourselves. Mebbe we should have . . . ' He swung back to the barred window. 'I heard a sound out there, damnit!'

'And I heard one the other side of this door,' croaked Frank. 'Who's goin' to make it first?'

★   ★   ★

Larsen's men spread thick and fast through the town, splitting into groups to search and ransack with systematic progress from one end of the main street to the other, leaving nothing that was habitable or might be a hiding place unchecked.

Homes, shops, stores, sheds — even the scatterings of empty crates, barrels and water butts — were probed, turned over, entered, broken open, their contents tossed and thrown aside for the merest hint of a presence that smelled of, or suggested, gunfighter.

Folk stood shudderingly aside as the

men stomped and clattered into their homes with faint regard for the fate or value of the contents, speed and thoroughness being their only concern; shivered at the sounds of broken crockery, furniture dragged and pushed aside, chests and drawers tipped to the floor, smashed and splintered, carpets lifted, drapes dragged from their hangings, the sidekicks' voices, cackling laughter, sneers and mocking curses ringing in their ears until, with a final flurry of abuse, the men would pass on to the next target and begin again, the frenzy of the search festering like a growth.

Few raised a hand or word in protest, those who did being cuffed or flung to the dirt for their trouble, some personal item of the home crushed underfoot, deliberately smashed, sometimes pocketed with no more than a vindictive smirk behind a snarled curse.

Townsmen sweated and mouthed silently, women sobbed, young ones clung wild-eyed and pale. A girl still in her teens raged against her best dress being trampled across the dirt, only to be grabbed, spun among the sidekicks like a joint of meat to be gnawed at and slobbered over till she collapsed in a scratched, half-naked heap and the dress was thrown mockingly over her.

Abe Cartwright's store was torn apart, but not before the raiders had helped themselves to whatever took their eye and the windows had been smashed. The barbering shop fared no better in the momentum of a destruction that rose steadily, inevitably to a senseless pitch as the fever of it gripped and the sidekicks passed into hell-bent mayhem, no longer aware who or what they were looking for.

Only a matter of time, thought Doc McLean from the porch of his trashed home, before the appeal of wanton destruction ran its course and the sidekicks' attentions turned to sating their thirsts and tumbling that night to the abyss of violent orgy.

He swallowed, grabbed his bag and strode into the street, his gaze darting to left and right, mind in a whirl of the bodies to be comforted, cuts and bruises to be tended, but a part of it still levelled enough to wonder if Billhook had made it to the back of the Trailbender, if Ship O'Toole was holding his own there in the saloon bar and his eyes still tight on Larsen.

Wondering too if, in the scrambling heap of shadows surrounding him, the next one to grow and lunge would be the only one he wanted to see.

Doc had reached the girl hugging the rags of the best dress to her, when the sidekicks gathered to catch their breath, their gleaming gazes searching like the eyes of hungry buzzards for the next likely prey. Might be the livery, he thought, or would they get to rounding up the women? No saying where the anger might be fanned on the next whim of the breeze.

An elderly man broke from the group of townfolk and staggered towards the raiders, an axe handle whirling above his head.

'Sons-of-all-the-goddam-bitches!' he screamed. 'I'll break the heads of every last one of yuh!'

'Get back!' yelled another man. 'Get back, yuh hear?'

But the man staggered on, sweat-soaked, shuddering, his curses rolling to a growling pitch, the axe handle cleaving the air.

Doc rose slowly from his knees, a cold chill churning miserably in the pit of his stomach as he watched the sidekicks turn to the man, grins breaking like slivers of broken glass across their faces, hands already sliding and twitching to the butts of Colts.

'Oh, hell!' groaned Doc.

'Get back, damn yuh!' screamed somebody from the shadows.

'Keep comin', old fella!' shouted one of the sidekicks. 'We all want a shot at yuh. Fill that bent body of yours with more holes than — '

The blazing roar of the shots seemed

to rip through the darkest depths of the night as if the moon itself had spat them.

And four men lay dead before anyone could blink.

★ ★ ★

Doc gulped as if choking on a slab of the silence that followed the drifting, haunting echo of the shots. The old man stood frozen in his steps, his eyes wide and watering, mouth hanging open, the axe handle loose at his side in a slack, bony grip. The sobbing girl fingered the rags of the dress. The townfolk stared, hardly seeming to breathe, their bodies stiff as silhouetted scare-crows against the soft shimmerings of lantern glow. And the sidekicks, motionless, not a limb moving, not a lip twitching, could only gaze as if seeing ghosts at the bodies strewn across the dirt where they had twisted into death.

Abe Cartwright was sodden to a mount of sweat on the shadowed boardwalk. 'Hell on earth,' he groaned on a thin, pinched swallow.

Jonas Whitman shuffled on his knees from the chaos of his barber's shop, his body suddenly cold as ice, his bones rattling.

Sheriff Tamms's eyes were focusing for the first time in days, his head thudding to the pound of a thunder that seemed to be closing.

Ship O'Toole had reached the batwings of the stifling bar, the butt of a glowing cigar scorching the tips of his fingers without him seeming to feel a thing.

The bar girls had huddled together like a nest of ruffled fledglings.

The drunk had stood witness to a night of the coming of the demons and dived face down in the dirt.

Doc shifted, grabbing his bag as he moved to the nearest of the bodies.

'Leave him where he is,' snapped a sidekick, a Colt tight and ranging in his grip, his narrowed gaze scanning wildly. 'Ain't nothin' yuh can do for him.'

'Seems like yuh mystery gunman's given yuh the slip again, don't it?' clipped Doc.

The sidekick's eyes fastened on Doc's face. 'Watch yuh mouth there. Bein' the pill roller round here don't give yuh no privileges.' He ranged the Colt through a swinging arc. 'Get the street cleared,' he yelled. 'All of yuh, get back to yuh homes. Don't show yuh faces 'til I say so. Yuh hear me? Now do it!' He stared at Doc again. 'And that includes you, McLean. Yuh won't be needed here.'

'Wouldn't bank on that,' mouthed Doc, shrugging his shoulders as he moved away to the girl with the dress.

'All right,' snapped the sidekick again, turning to his twitching, staring partners, 'so we know that scumbag's still around. Let's go burn the butt off the bastard!'

'Not so fast there,' croaked a bull-shouldered gunslinger, stepping to the soft glow of light. 'We just lost four good men here — *four*, damn it! Faster than squashin' sleepin' flies. And yuh can sure as hell bet the gun that took 'em out is fixed tight as a finger on every man here. We all move off this street, we get to eatin' dirt same as the others.'

The men grunted as their gazes came to life over the boardwalk, darkened windows, shadows beyond the lantern light, rooftops, alleys and half-lit corners.

'We goin' to let one gun — ' began the first sidekick again.

'Are you?' growled Bull-shoulders. 'Two more spits of that lead and we're down to a half of what stepped outa that bar not a few hours back.'

'So one of us gets to Larsen, hear how he wants us to handle this. You, you get to him, seein' as how yuh got such a mouth on yuh!'

Bull-shoulders spat, hitched his pants, drew his Colt and spun the chamber. 'So mebbe I will,' he shrugged. 'Mebbe that's just what the fella wants.'

The man eased away, his steps deliberate, measured, the gun casual at his side, his gaze steady on the boardwalk and the batwings ahead of him.

'Hidin' to hell he don't make the 'wings,' hissed a sidekick, scuffing a nervous boot.

'Hidin' to hell he don't make the boards!' hissed another.

'Shut it!' snapped a third.

Bull-shoulders was into the pool of light cast from the bar when the gun opened up again. But not at him.

The lead spread fast, accurate, spitting and snarling among the men still standing in the street. Two fell without a whispered sound; one staggered forward, blood bubbling at his throat, before hitting the dirt with a thud; a fourth spun, his eyes so wide and bulging they threatened to hit the ground ahead of him.

Only then did those still standing scatter to the shadows like scurrying ants.

Bull-shoulders crashed through the batwings, a groaning curse choking in his throat, his gaze emptying to a hollow stare as he took in the deserted bar.

17

The steps had been there, but approached unheard, as soft in their stealth as paws in no hurry; the silent, tight-faced figure reached the door, paused, listened, and waited a full minute before spreading the fingers of its gloved hand to the key and turning it.

Esme Green had heard nothing of the steps along the corridor, the deep, controlled breathing, click of the turned key — not so much as a whisper of sound in her intense concentration on what was happening in the street below the window.

She had seen the sidekicks begin their destructive onslaught on the homes and buildings, the townfolk gather in their haunted huddles, the ransacking of the store, the barber's shop; groaned at the mauling of the young girl and the growing fever in the men's search. She had known what was coming, where it might end.

But her view from the first-floor room above the saloon bar had also given her a sight of something others would have missed.

She had seen a crouched, dark figure moving through the shadows somewhere back of Doc McLean's place; watched it take a few careful steps, pause in the deepest darkness, move again, never in one place more than seconds, disregarding the activity in the street. A figure that seemed to limp through its movements, halt as if to gather its strength, wait on the easing of a surge of pain.

And for one brief, trembling moment then, her fingers spread nervously at the sweat in her neck, she had begun to wonder . . .

But the moment had passed, died in a sudden gasping swallow, an icy chill slithering down her spine, at the sound of the door opening, the creak of a floorboard to a step, the squeaking swing of a hinge as the door closed shut on a gentle click, and the slow rasp of breathing seemed to fill the room like an animal sniffing out its corners.

Esme's hands ran instinctively down the folds of the cheap dress, her fingers fumbling on the shape of the scissors held in the garter, pulling away to her back as her grip settled on the windowsill. She peered into the gloom, to the tall, stiffened reach of the man in the depths of it, the gleam of the split colour of his piercing eyes, parched, expressionless grey of his face.

'Time's come for you to earn yuh keep, lady.' The voice grated, slid like a crunching of disturbed pebbles, the lips slanted to a gap for it to slither through.

Esme backed, twitching on a shiver, the voices and clatter in the street below her drifting to long echoes. 'Go to hell,' she croaked, the words cracked and splintered.

The polished leather of Larsen's boot creaked as he shifted his weight. One

184

hand slid to his thigh, the fingers tapping silently. 'Been there, and back, more than once,' he mouthed quietly. 'Bet you ain't, though. Nothin' like, eh? Figured all this for as bad as it gets. Lady, yuh ain't seen nothin' yet!'

Esme flinched as he creaked a step closer.

'I want yuh down there in the street, yuh hear? I want yuh seen, so whoever it is pricklin' at my side with that fancy shootin' of his gets to understandin' exactly what he's condemnin' if he don't back off.'

Another creak, another step.

'And in case that ain't to his persuadin', I got three of them sodbustin' neighbours of yours locked in the storeroom. Know what I plan for them, lady? Yuh got the vaguest notion spillin' round that pretty head?'

Esme shivered at the tricklings of cold sweat in her neck, fumbled her fingers for the touch of the scissors.

'I'll tell yuh. I plan on takin' them back to their spreads, tyin' them tight to their porches, then lettin' the boys raise hell with the biggest torchin' the Utepan's ever seen. One by one, their womenfolk and kin watchin' on.' The voice shuddered on a rasp of breath. 'What yuh reckon, lady?'

Esme's mouth opened, but the sound died in her throat.

'Won't be necessary in your case, o'course,' Larsen sneered on, 'seein' as how you're already a widow.' He paused to hiss through his teeth. 'Shame yuh fella took to that fool plan to ride to Carver. Real shame. Sent two of my best boys to settle with him. Still . . . there's a whole new future pannin' out for you. Play it my way, and we're goin' to be spendin' a whole lot of time together.' He hissed again. 'Takin' yuh as an extra payment for all my hard work out here. Railroad don't provide them sorta comforts.'

Esme brushed at the sting of tears on her cheeks, licked her lips and stiffened. 'Don't get to bankin' on one spit — ' she had half croaked when the gunfire shattered the night at her back like the crack of high storm breaking a heat-wave, and Larsen had pushed her aside in his lunge for the window.

★   ★   ★

That same roar and blaze had silenced the three men locked in the Trailbender storeroom and lifted the trembling guts of their stomachs to their mouths.

Joe Medley fell back from the barred window, a look of astonishment creasing his cobweb-streaked face. Henry Keyes was suddenly unaware of the pain in his wounded arm, the bloodstained fingers gripping it. 'What the hell!' were the only hissed words he could croak as he widened his eyes on the gloom. Frank Cooper had flinched, pulled back from his vigil of listening at the locked door and stared blankly.

'Sonofabitch — yuh hear that?' Joe had gulped. 'Only one gun hereabouts rips lead that fast.'

'T'ain't possible,' Henry had murmured vaguely, blinking as the echoes of the gunfire whined on the night.

Frank had crept slowly towards the door again, his gaze levelled and steady on the knob, certain now that it could only be a matter of seconds before it turned and whoever it was out there . . .

But he was off his guard and gasping on a choked breath as the door swung open, crashing into his face, and the bulk of a whiskey-soured sidekick loomed in the space, a Colt cleaving the air like a gleaming eye searching for a target to settle on.

'Out!' growled the man. 'Now — and the first to twitch is dead meat.'

Henry had come unsteadily upright, Joe groaned and squirmed in the sweat-soaked chill of his shirt, Frank shook his throbbing head and had taken two staggering steps to the corridor that led to the bar when a thud, a clang of iron to steel, splintering of timber, groaning curse of effort, sent a rush of night air swirling into the room.

The back door to the rear of the saloon hung frail as a broken wing on its hinges, the shattered planking a tangle of hanging membranes, the air pungent with the smell of cordite and drifting wisps of gunsmoke misting the towering thrust of Billhook as he hacked his way into the gloom, caught the gleam of the Colt in his gaze, the gnarled, knotted face of the sidekick, and hurled the iron-headed hammer into the man's groin.

The sidekick groaned, bent double, the gun spinning from his grip to the blacksmith's feet. Seconds later there was the roar of a single shot, a throttled scream and nothing more of Larsen's man than the agonized twist of his body for Joe Medley to stare at.

'They got Mrs Green upstairs,' grunted Billhook, tossing the Colt to Frank as he retrieved the hammer to his giant grip. 'Let's go! Watch for Larsen.'

They pounded, slid, skidded down

the corridor, broke in a tide of limbs into the bar and almost collided in a heap at the sight of the bull-shouldered sidekick hovering nervously at the batwings.

'Damn!' spluttered Joe, already diving for the cover of an upturned table.

'Frank — the gun! Use it, f'Cris'sake!' yelled Henry, spinning helplessly to the bar, his wounded arm oozing fresh blood.

It took Frank Cooper the better part of five seconds to level the Colt in his shaking hand, for his focus to clear behind the blur of sweat and still smoky haze of the bar; seconds in which Bull-shoulders might so easily have levelled his own piece and blazed a full chamber of lead — and not missed.

Frank should have been crumpling to the floor, his trigger finger barely into taking up the pressure, breath tight in his chest, but he was still standing, eyes as bulbous as a basking toad's, when the spitting rage of gunfire from the boardwalk beyond the batwings hit Bull-shoulders, square in the back of his neck.

Frank's shot, when it finally left the barrel, buried itself in a man already dead.

'Who the hell fired that?' croaked Joe, struggling from the cover of the table.

'Don't matter none, does it?' snapped Billhook, heading for the stairs. 'It's Mrs Green we gotta look to.'

He was three steps into the climb to the floor above him, one hand gripping a banister, the other the iron-head hammer, when he halted, bared chest heaving, sweat beading thick on his brow, at the drift of the shape on the landing.

'Mrs Green — yuh all right?' he murmured.

'Esme?' said Joe, coming slowly to the foot of the stairs.

'Goddamn it, gal, what the hell they done to yuh?' groaned Henry.

Billhook sprinted on to Esme's side, took her arm and led her gently down the stairs to the bar.

'Where's Larsen?' frowned Frank. 'Yuh seen him?'

Esme shuddered and slid to Billhook's bulk for her balance. 'I seen him,' she whispered. 'He was right here, in that room up there.'

'He still there?' asked Joe.

'Heard the shootin', took one look at the street, and left. Just disappeared. Just like that.'

'Hell!' cursed Frank. 'Sonofabitch could be anywhere. Mebbe we should — '

'No,' snapped Billhook. 'We don't do nothin'. We stay right here, right where we are. Leave it.'

'*Leave it?*' flared Joe. 'Let Larsen round up them rats of his and come stormin' back here? Hell, fella, we won't be worth no more than dirt under his boots! And who we leavin' it to, f'Cris-sake?'

There was another blaze and roar of

shots from the street.

'Him,' said Billhook, his gaze turning to the batwings and the depths of the gunsmoke-misted night. 'Whoever he is.'

18

The early morning light came slow and furtive to the main street of Mission, like a stranger seeing it for the first time, pausing among shadows, slipping silently to corners. The silence too seemed out of place, as if dropped there by accident, something discarded, the echoes of gunfire, shouts and screams and curses long since faded.

The stranger might, in fact, have reckoned for Mission being a ghost town at that early hour, with the sun no more than a haze to skim the dawn chill and fingers of soft mist — until, that is, he reached the boardwalk to the Trailbender saloon, the fretted darkness of the batwings and the flicker of thin-flamed lanterns beyond them.

Things were a whole lot different there among the tensed, expectant faces and the tired but still fearful eyes that stared from them.

Doc McLean, the wisps of his white hair scattered like dust across his brow, was on his feet facing the assembled townfolk, Frank Cooper, Henry Keyes and Joe Medley seated at a table to his left, Esme Green, the bar girl outfit exchanged for her own home dress and comforting shawl, her eyes hollowed and dark, cheeks ashen, to his right. Ship O'Toole, Abe Cartwright and Jonas Whitman stood with their backs to the bar. Billhook had settled himself on the stairs, the iron-head hammer at his side, the bar girls ranged behind him. Sheriff Tamms sulked in a shadowed corner.

'No, yuh ain't dreamin',' announced Doc, his gaze tight on the gathering, 'they're gone, them that ain't waitin' on burial scattered, Lord knows where, but gone. We seen the last of 'em, and that includes Larsen. He won't be back.'

Somebody sighed. A small group muttered cheerfully among themselves. A man with a bruised, blackening eye leaned back in a chair and stared at the ceiling. Esme stifled a shiver.

'But we're all standin' in the mess of it, ain't we? Witness to what we allowed to happen, stood back from, never lifted a finger to fight against — '

'Where is he, Doc?' shouted a man from the back of the bar. 'And just who was that fella with the gun? That's what we wanna hear.'

The gathering muttered its agreement. 'He's right, Doc,' called one. 'We gotta know. Damn it, if it hadn't been for him — '

'All right, all right,' said Doc, raising his arms for silence. 'I'll tell yuh what I know, but it ain't much, and that's gospel. Fella sneaked into my place middle of the night some days back. Real bad shape he was in too. Lead buried in a wound weeks old. Didn't say how he'd come by it, and I weren't for askin' — he weren't the sorta fella yuh asked a deal of — just said as how some homesteaders had brought him outa the Utepan to the Green spread

196

and done their best by him. Said he'd figured for the homesteaders bein' in a whole heap of trouble and that he weren't for addin' to it, and in any case . . . '

Doc paused a moment, his gaze darkening. 'In any case, he knew Larsen, knew the scum's reckonin' and it wouldn't do nobody a spit of good if Larsen found him bein' nursed by Mrs Green here.'

Esme stifled another shiver.

'So he pulled out,' added Doc. 'Headed for my place — and he sure as hell needed lookin' to!'

'He fire that shot the day they buried Charlie Bishop?' asked a red-faced man twirling his hat in his hands.

'He did,' said Doc.

'Ride out trackin' them two fellas Larsen sent to the Carver Trail?' croaked an old-timer.

'That, too,' said Doc.

'And he sure as hell got busy last night!' chimed Joe Medley, wiping a hand over his face.

'So where's he now?' said a young man from among a group gathered at the batwings. 'He ain't holed-up your place, is he, Doc? Probably ain't even in town. So where'd he go? He just ridden out, disappeared? He in any real shape to go anyplace?'

'Better shape than he was when I first clapped eyes on him,' answered Doc. 'But yuh right, he ain't here, not to my knowledge, anyhow. He mebbe figures we got the measure of this situation. He knows for a fact Clyde Green's goin' to make it to Carver City — knows it 'cus he made sure he kept goin'. Told me as much. Clyde'll be back here in a day or so and you can lay measure to it, and a whole posse of help along of him.'

Esme laid her cheek to the hand Doc placed on her shoulder, a soft smile and sigh of relief trembling at her lips.

'That's fine, Doc,' croaked the old-timer, settling a wad of baccy between his stained teeth, 'and there ain't a body here not grateful to hear as how Clyde Green's still breathin' and

198

likely as not goin' to get this whole railroad mess sorted. Townfolk here ain't done much to aid in that, and we own to it, fair and square. Somethin' we're goin' to have to live with and shape ourselves up better for the future.

'*But* — and I'm speakin' here for every man standin' — what about Larsen? Yuh say as how yuh reckon he won't be back. Mebbe yuh right. Got a lot to answer to, ain't he, 'specially when his paymasters and the law get to hearin' of what went on here? But you really believe that, Doc? You sayin' as how yuh don't figure for a man like Larsen seekin' his revenge? Takes a generous soul to see it like that, don't it?'

Doc swallowed. 'Well, mebbe it does,' he began. 'But I still say — '

The old-timer sucked noisily on the wad. 'Way I see it, we got one almighty tall question to ask ourselves: was that stranger with the fast gun payin' back his debt to the homesteaders when he took this town apart single-handed, or was it Larsen he wanted? Well, he's settled with the homesteaders, sure enough, but he ain't with Larsen, has he, not if that sonofabitch is still out there? And if Larsen gets to headin' back this way . . . '

'Hell!' mouthed Frank Cooper.

'A bloodbath,' hissed O'Toole behind the mask of billowing cigar smoke.

'Sonofabitch,' grunted Abe Cartwright.

Billhook took the handle of the hammer in one hand and weighed the head in the other.

Sheriff Tamms began to shake.

The bar girls huddled like a hatching of chicks.

The others sat in silence as if the spreading lift of the early morning light through Mission might bring a whisper they would miss.

* * *

It was late in the afternoon of that day when the homesteaders cleared the town and returned to their spreads, Frank, Joe and Henry to the welcoming relief and delight of their families, Esme, once she had washed up and eaten, told her story and relaxed in the comforts of the Medley home — and in spite of Nancy's insistence that she should stay over — to her own place.

The loneliness of the spread without Clyde had scant appeal, but she needed she felt, to be there. 'Heaven knows,' she had smiled against protests and young Sarah's persistent tugging at her skirts, 'don't want that man of mine ridin' in to a deserted home. Might figure for me gettin' up to no good!'

But there had been a deeper, gnawing reason for finally waving a cheerful goodnight to Joe once he had seen her safely home: she needed to figure through for herself in her own time and space, those last minutes of being alone in the room at the Trailbender with Larsen. Needed to see again that last look on his face as he had pulled back from the window, the gunfire echoing on the groans and scattering of his sidekicks, and stared into her face, his hauntingly coloured eyes seeming to peel back the skin.

She had thought in those shuddering, shadow choking moments that Larsen might reach for her, run those groping gloved hands of his over her neck until they settled at her throat and he strangled the life out of her. Or perhaps he would draw on that Colt and simply shoot her where she cowered, one hand still feeling for the touch of the scissors in the garter.

But he had only stared without blinking, waiting it seemed for interminable minutes before glancing quickly at the window again and moving, as if no more than a shadow, to the door.

'This ain't done yet,' he had mouthed, the eyes suddenly bright as flames. 'I'll be back. You be watchin' on it.'

Would he, she wondered now, her gaze empty on the sprawl of the land from the homestead? Would he lurk out there, maybe on the bleak fringes of the Utepan where a man could hide, survive on the meanest pickings and pass undetected for weeks and months? Would he be watching for Clyde's return, and then, at some misty morning hour before sun-up, ride in to seek his revenge? Or would the slow scuff of hoofs through dirt come at nightfall?

Or would the gunfighter be there ahead of him?

And just where, she frowned, had he disappeared to? Ridden north, picked up any one of a dozen trails out of Mission, his mind content in the routing of Larsen and his sidekicks, 'payment' duly made to the homesteaders for saving his life, nursing him through the worst of his wound?

Or did it all go a whole lot deeper between him and Larsen? Had the gunfighter been heading this way intent for some reason on a showdown? Was he still waiting on that day?

Maybe she should have said more to Doc McLean, told him of Larsen's threat, told Frank and Joe and Henry. Or maybe they too had their fears and doubts. Maybe every man in Mission had been living in the shadow of Larsen long enough to know it would not fade overnight.

But once Clyde was back, once the lawmen, land agents and railroad company men were here . . .

Even so, she thought, when the sprawl of the land lay to the first evening shadows, she would go look out that old shotgun of Clyde's, load it, keep it to hand wherever she went. Best not get to taking risks.

Esme's closing thoughts to the drift of sleep on that night had not been of Clyde, of the room at the Trailbender, not even of Larsen, but of the man who had lain seemingly lifeless all those days on the bed in the spare room, and the one brief moment when he had opened his eyes as if seeing far beyond the four walls and the neatly draped window.

Where had he been then, Esme had wondered; who had he seen?

19

'Give it another day. No tellin' how it's goin' for him out there. Might be a heap of ends to tie up, folk to see, papers to look to. Damn it, Esme, there's just no sayin' what Clyde's had to face at Carver. Only certainty is, he's there, and yuh can bet yuh sweet life doin' his best by everyone. Sure to be. Yuh see that, don't yuh?'

Doc McLean eased in the saddle to the shift of his mount as it tossed its head and turned his careful gaze to the troubled face of Esme Green where she sat her horse at his side on the sunlit edge of the slope to the distant Utepan.

Not easy for her, he thought, watching as her eyes squinted yet again on the glare as if probing every rock, every drift of dirt on the worn straggle of trail. Bad enough Clyde riding out like he had, chancing his arm the full length of its reach; worse when it came to her being taken hostage by Larsen, subjected to whatever it was squirmed back of his warped mind.

And now, only the hours of waiting on her man's return, riding out here like she did every opportunity offered, on every whim of an excuse she would find, to simply watch, wait, and maybe pray on the hope of that first lift of a dust cloud as riders approached.

'I know, I hear what yuh sayin', Doc,' sighed Esme, lifting a hand to shadow her gaze, 'and you're right. It's just that — '

'Damn it, Esme, we all appreciate how yuh feelin' — ain't a man not sweatin' on the same sight yuh waitin' on — but we just gotta be patient, give it time, try seein' it the way Clyde must be facin' it. He'll be here, real soon. Meantime, I ain't restin' easy with the thought of yuh bein' alone out here. Billhook's all for joinin' yuh 'til Clyde's back. Says as how he can organize for somebody to take over at the livery for a day or so. And I'm all for it. There's gotta be a man along of yuh — and I ain't just thinkin' of him choppin' wood and lookin' to yuh stock. There's other considerations.'

Doc's careful gaze had glinted a shade tighter on Esme's face, his hands taken a fresh hold on the reins.

'Yuh referrin' there to Larsen, aren't you?' asked Esme, still squinting.

'He's a factor we gotta keep in mind,' said Doc gently. 'I ain't for sayin' he's still about. If he's got a spit of sense he'll be long gone, far as he can get, fast as he can. But 'sense' in his book don't figure the same as it does in mine. Wouldn't like to say for certain where he is, and that's a risk I ain't for takin'.' He gripped the reins. 'Billhook'll be here at sundown.'

Esme sighed again as she lowered her hand from her eyes. 'And the gun-fighter? What about him?'

It was Doc's turn to sigh. 'Just no knowin', is there? Ain't clapped eyes on hair or hide of him since the shootin'.

Didn't see a deal of him through that, save that I knew he'd slipped clear of that upstairs room at my place he'd been occupyin'. Never said a word of himself; never no name, why he was here, where he'd come from, where he'd taken the lead in the shootin', or why, and he sure as hell didn't give one lick of a notion where he might be headin' — *if* he's headed anywhere.'

'Yuh mean he might still be around?' frowned Esme.

Doc shrugged. 'Who's to know? Fellas of his style go their own ways in their own time to whatever instincts tell 'em, though God knows where a man gets to holin'-up in a land like we're seein' out there. Most wouldn't last two days.'

They sat in easy silence for a moment, their gazes steady, hands soft on loose reins, thoughts drifting, gathering, but left unspoken.

'Time I was movin',' said Doc at last. 'Go take a look at Henry Keyes' arm then get back to town. More than enough to keep me busy there!' He adjusted his hat. 'Shall I ride with yuh back to your place?'

'No, I'll mebbe stay on out here a while,' smiled Esme. 'But thanks, Doc. I'll be fine, don't you fret.'

Doc grunted, turned his mount through a half circle and shortened the reins. 'Can't say I won't, but it'll help knowin' Billhook's with yuh.'

Esme was still watching the sprawl of the empty trail to the Utepan long after Doc had disappeared.

★ ★ ★

Some miles apart on the same morning that Doc McLean was muttering consoling words to Henry Keyes as he dressed and bandaged the homesteader's wounded arm, Joe Medley was talking to himself through a long scan of the spread of his land at its easternmost reaches.

'Parched,' he had murmured more than once, running a hand over his mount's ears. 'Dry as a dog's scorched bone.' And probably set to get a deal worse before the rainy season finally arrived. Some weeks away, he thought, lifting his narrowed eyes to the cloudless blue of the high, endless sky and the burning ball of the sun. Sight too hot with it. Fellow could come close to exhaustion out there — fellow fool enough to linger, that is. Sort of fellow who might be on the run, or intent on staying hidden.

Damn it, he groaned, there he went again, letting his imagination get the better of him, figuring for somebody like Larsen — somebody very like Larsen, in fact — being out there, holed up, waiting on his chance, the moment when he might . . .

Trouble was — unless his tired, watery, sun-pinched eyes were deceiving him — there *was* somebody out there, or had been, and not too long back neither.

That drift of land, where it rose to a length of rocky ridge and shelved to a narrow gully, somebody had been there, sure enough; could still see the embers of the low fire, horse dung and scuffed dirt.

Almost smell the fellow, thought Joe, minutes later as he reined his mount closer and slid slowly from the saddle. Only one man, one horse; simple fire, nothing to raise a billow of black smoke; place where a blanket had been stretched, a body eased to its full length, rested up, but maybe not slept.

No, definitely not slept. Sleeping men sometimes never got to waking.

Joe squatted to the embers and ran his fingers through them. Still warm from the night before, he judged, but the fellow had moved on early, probably before first light. He came upright again and turned to where the hoof scuffs trailed away. Not heading deeper east, he reckoned. In fact, when he came to look at it, the rider had moved out as if trailing the very boundary of Joe's spread on a south-westerly course.

Two or three hours of holding to a

track in that direction would bring him to . . . Where, wondered Joe, squinting on the shimmering glare?

Fellow would have passed Frank Cooper's place soon after sun-up, followed the line of the scrub to the south, and then, if he had a mind for it, trailed far side of Charlie Bishop's burned-out barn, lifted on the easy drift west and had . . . the Green homestead clear in his sights only a mile or so on.

The sweat in Joe's shirt was thick and clinging as he mounted up again and gave the horse its head in a fast gallop towards the Cooper spread.

★ ★ ★

He found Frank Cooper in a thoughtful, pensive mood, standing deep in the shadows of the lean-to at the distant end of his corral, his fingers scratching lazily at his chin, his gaze flicking over the marks in the sand at his feet.

'Yuh seein' there what I think yuh

seein'?' said Joe, reining short, dismounting and hitching his horse.

'Yuh seen somethin' similar?' asked Frank.

'Back there. Know what I reckon? Tell yuh, straight up. We got Larsen slitherin' round us like a rattler.'

Frank's hand fell from his chin to hook the thumb in his belt. 'Passed this way sun-up, I'd reckon, but then he turned directly north, out the Utepan way.'

'The Utepan?' frowned Joe. 'I'd figured him for Clyde's spread and us gettin' over there fast.'

Frank scuffed a boot through the dirt and lifted his gaze to the heat-hazed distance of the horizon. 'North,' he repeated. 'Wouldn't have touched the Green place. But no sayin' for certain it is Larsen, is there? Nothin' here to say so.'

'That gunfighter?' said Joe.

'Mebbe. And if it was . . . well, he ain't driftin' here-abouts for his health, is he?'

214

'Could be he reckons on Larsen bein' close. Could be he's plannin' on a showdown with him. Hell, could be we might be slap in the middle of it!'

'Or,' murmured Frank, his gaze shifting back to Joe, 'it could be that Larsen will be lookin' for a last edge, settin' out to bag two birds in the same swoop.'

'Esme?' swallowed Joe. 'Get to her somehow, then wait — '

But Joe's voice had already faded on Frank's back as the homesteader strode away to saddle up, his shadow leaping ahead of him like the sudden threat in a storm-laden cloud.

20

Waiting, always waiting, Esme had fumed as she thundered her mount from the sprawl of the Utepan back to the homestead. Story of her life, damn it! Waiting on hope, waiting on help, for Clyde's return; waiting on the swish of picks and shovels, clang of iron as a railroad came to life, waiting on the slim chance that it might never come to pass.

Well, she was all through with waiting, as of now! She was back to the doing.

She would set to work, do the jobs about the spread she could handle, spruce the place up, so that by the time Billhook rode in . . .

So much for the firm resolve, she thought a half-hour later, the homestead door thudding shut to her weight as she slumped against it and brushed angrily at the smear of fresh tears on her cheeks. She could no more get to concentrating on doing jobs about the place than she could on fencing her thoughts. Where was Clyde now; how long before he skirted the 'Pan; who would be with him?

But supposing he had never made it to Carver; what if he was stiffening out there on the trail right now, waiting on scavenging beaks and talons ripping him to pieces?

She brushed at another flood of tears, sniffed loudly and blinked on the blur of shafting light through the rear wall window. Sun was already high and hot, the land scorching, the air thick and unmoving; not a sound, nothing stirring.

Or was there?

Could be the state of mind she was in, of course, or the pounding ache behind her eyes, but had that been a movement out there she had heard, a soft, slow, measured step, a boot barely touching dirt as it approached from the wood store?

Was she willing the silence to break, for the step to be Clyde, one of the neighbours? Had being held back there at the Trailbender shredded her nerves to the quick?

'Try me!' she mouthed, stiffening her shoulders as she slid across the room to the window.

Nobody there. Wood store door tight shut. Mounts in the open-fronted stabling quiet enough. Shadows thick and dark as fallen pines. Definitely nobody there.

She swung round at a noise from the main bedroom. 'Hell!' she hissed, her eyes dancing wildly now for something to take in her hands.

Nothing within reach. She had left the shotgun under her bed, damn it!

She moved on, sidling round the bulge of the stone fireplace, to the wall flanking the bedroom door, stared at the knob as if expecting it to turn, stretched a hand towards it, the fingers trembling and suddenly chilled.

Dare she? But what if —

The door was open and the space filled by the looming bulk and gleaming stare of Larsen before Esme had blinked and the fingers retreated.

'Some unfinished business here, lady,' sneered Larsen on a hiss of his hot, tainted breath, the strange eyes seeming to retreat behind a curtain of darkness. 'Yuh make one sound and you're dead.'

Esme shuddered and backed to the wall as Larsen's tight, eager gaze took in the room, the door to the veranda standing open, the windows white and wide to the blazing light, the shadows stiff, the silence oppressive on the slow, mournful tick of the clock.

She watched, cold in the cling of a trickling sweat, stiffened at the thud of the door closing under Larsen's boot, swish of the drapes against the light, and swallowed on a dry, hollow throat as Larsen turned to face her again.

'Now we wait,' he drawled. 'In silence.'

Esme slid carefully along the wall. 'Wait?' she croaked. 'What we waitin' on? There ain't nothin' — '

'We wait on that sonofabitch with the free-rangin' Colt. He'll be here. Or mebbe that sodbustin' husband of yours'll make it first. Don't matter none, does it? Far as either of 'em's going once they're here.' Larsen's eyes gleamed. 'We wait. Understand?'

Esme's stare was as cold as the chill in her bones. Sure, she thought, she knew all about waiting, maybe far more than Larsen. She could wait for as long as it took, and this she reminded herself was her territory, not Ship O'Toole's private room at the Trailbender.

'Yuh relax there, yuh hear?' said Larsen, fingering a drape aside to the merest chink for his quick glance to the paddock and sprawl of the corral. 'Meantime, this dump run to a drink? Yuh man got a bottle stashed some place?'

Esme's hands fluttered nervously at

her sides. 'There's whiskey,' she murmured.

'Get it,' snapped Larsen, leaning into another glance to the paddock.

Esme sidled on to the cabinet at the back of the room, fumbled a door open and slid a wet, sticky hand to the half-empty bottle in the corner, her fingers hesitating before they finally gripped. There was something else there, a shape, familiar to the touch, left where it had always lived.

This was her territory.

Larsen was still glancing, licking at his cracked, sunburned lips, when Esme placed the bottle on the table and eased back again to the cabinet.

Now it was all down to the waiting.

★ ★ ★

'Esme's horse hitched there, but she ain't alone,' whispered Joe into Frank Cooper's ear where they sprawled in the hot, shadowed dirt on the eastern ridge over-looking the Green spread. 'I can smell she ain't.'

Frank grunted and spat the gritty sand from between his teeth. 'Drapes drawn, door closed, on a day like this, and her watchin' for Clyde — don't make sense.' He spat again. 'Yuh right, she ain't alone. So who's with her?'

'Hidin' to nothin', it's Larsen.' Joe groaned and clawed his fingers through the dirt. 'How the hell we goin' — ?'

'If yuh thinkin' on how we're goin' to get to Esme there, think again. We ain't.' Frank slapped his lips on another spit. 'Doc might still be over Henry's place. One of us should get to him. Mebbe he can raise some help in town. One of us stays here, watchin'. Ain't a deal else to do, not 'til we got some hands here and we figure out how to get to Esme before Larsen turns his gun on her.'

'Mebbe he'll bargain,' said Joe.

'For what? Only thing he wants is the satisfaction of a killin'.'

'Goddamn it!' mouthed Joe, sliding away from the ridge. 'Don't you move none 'til I get back. And if that scumbag down there — '

'He won't,' sighed Frank. 'Got all he wants for now, ain't he?'

* * *

Larsen swigged steadily from the bottle, swallowed long and deep, licked his tongue round the neck and twitched a grubby forefinger at the drapes. A shaft of sunlight burned for a moment over the washed green eye before the lid hooded it and the stare tightened. He murmured softly to himself, stepped clear of the window and slid the bottle to the table, the stare suddenly dark again as it settled on Esme.

'Yuh expectin' company?' he asked, his weight easing to one hip, thumbs to the drift of his belt. 'One of them neighbours, Doc McLean, somebody from town? Who's lookin' to yuh?'

Esme bit on a dry, trembling lip and dug the tips of her fingers into the wall at her back. 'Ain't nobody,' she croaked. 'I can manage.'

'Liar,' sneered Larsen. 'So who's the body sprawled out there on the ridge? That Joe Medley, Frank Cooper?'

'You're the one doin' the lookin',' flushed Esme. 'You tell me!'

Larsen's fingers flexed like claws. 'Don't get sassy, lady. I ain't in the mood for it.'

The sweat surged at Esme's neck as she tossed her hair and wiped what might have been a trickle of a tear from her cheek. 'Mebbe it's that fella yuh waitin' on,' she clipped, her voice strained but sharp. 'You accounted for him yet?'

'Oh,' frowned Larsen, 'and just who might that be? Not somebody yuh happened to cross by chance? Yuh seen him? He been here?'

'Sure he has,' said Esme stiffening. 'Right there, back of yuh. The spare room. He was there 'til ... ' She hesitated, the fingers tightening into the palms of her hands. ' 'Til he was good and ready.'

'He say anythin'?' snapped Larsen.

'Them vermin sidekicks yuh had along of yuh had good chance to hear if he had. Fella was here the night yuh passed on yuh three-week warnin', night yuh burned out Charlie Bishop's barn and murdered him. Mule-heads, weren't they? Not a grain of sense between 'em! Same might be said — '

Esme's flaring words, the pitch of her voice, had brought Larsen from the far end of the table to her side, the quick flash of his fingers to grab a handful of her hair and drag her face to within a breath of his slanted lips, the ghost-cold eyes.

'Yuh got some explaining to do here, lady. And now!' he snarled.

The gloom, the thickening heat of the room, and Larsen's sweating concentration on Esme, had been the luck of opportunity the shape easing towards the wood-shed had needed. It had merged unseen and soundless into the shadows.

And now it, too, waited.

225

21

They gathered, sweat-stained, anxious, lathered mounts hitched in the scatterings of lean shade, a mile beyond the Green spread and waited tense and twitchy on Doc McLean's orders.

'We all here?' he said, his gaze ranging quickly over the faces gathered round him.

'Many as is worth havin',' quipped Abe Cartwright, nursing his bandaged arm.

Doc counted out the heads: Abe, Jonas Whitman, Billhook, Ship O'Toole, Joe Medley, Frank Cooper, a pale-faced Henry Keyes. 'Good enough,' he grunted. 'Goin' to have to be.' He drew himself to his full height. 'Right, so let's get to the plannin'. Frank here's been keepin' a watch on the place while we got ourselves t'gether, and yuh heard what he says of how

226

things are back there. Home's shuttered up and silent. Larsen ain't in no hurry.'

'Quiet as the grave,' added Frank. 'If yuh take my meanin',' he flustered, skimming a boot cap to the dirt.

'Ain't no sayin' as to Esme, though, is there?' frowned O'Toole, rolling an unlit cigar through his fingers. 'God alone knows what she's sufferin', 'specially after bein' held like she was at my place. If yuh ask me — '

'Blast the head off the sonofabitch where he stands!' growled Henry.

'Hang him — real slow!' said Jonas, cracking his fingers as he licked at the sweat on his lips.

'Yeah, yeah,' soothed Doc, raising his arms, 'I hear yuh and know how yuh feel. All of a mind on that score, ain't we? But it's Esme we gotta look to. She's first and last in this if Clyde's efforts are worth a spit.'

'Always assumin' Clyde's efforts ain't been wasted.'

'Always assumin' Clyde's still

breathin',' drawled O'Toole darkly.

'He is,' snapped Doc. 'Just know he is. Could ride in any time. But meanwhile — '

'We do it like I figured,' said Billhook from the depths of the shade. 'Spoken to Doc here and he agrees. We go blastin' and blunderin' into that spread and Esme's as good as dead before she can draw breath.'

'What yuh have in mind?' murmured Frank.

'I ride in there alone — no guns, nothin' — just like I was passin' and callin' to help out.'

'Yuh reckon on Larsen fallin' for that?' sneered O'Toole.

Doc stepped forward, hands gripping the lapels of his coat. 'We all know why Larsen's there. He's waitin' on that gunfighter. Railroads, sodbusters . . . they don't figure no more. He's through on that score and knows it. What he's waitin' on now is personal, and he sure as hell ain't for drawin' attention to himself wastin' lead on a two-bit town's blacksmith. No, he'll want Billhook snaffled tight, sure enough, but once he's in there along of Esme, well, at least she'll have somebody standin' to her.'

'And the rest of us, what'll we be doin'?' winced Abe, cradling the wounded arm.

'We'll surround the place,' said Doc. 'We give it time, see if Clyde turns up, wait on that gunfighter makin' a move. But if he don't, come evenin', we step in, face on, take the place best we can, any way we're able. Billhook's job'll be to protect Esme.'

There was a moment of brittle silence.

'Who is this gunfighter, anyhow?' asked Joe. 'All I know is we dragged him half dead outa the 'Pan. What about you, Doc? You been closest to him. Who is he, f'Cris'sake?'

'I wish I knew,' murmured Doc. 'Or mebbe it's better I don't.'

'He about?' whispered Henry. 'Some place out there?'

'Your guess is as good as mine, Henry.'

But Doc had never been much for setting a deal of store on guesswork.

* * *

'Sonofa-snoopin'-bitch!' Larsen swung away from the window, his back to the door, and stared icily into Esme's face. 'Yuh got a visitor. We 'entertaining', or shall I gun this dumbhead blacksmith now?'

Esme shivered in spite of the stifling heat of the room, the thick, heavy shadows, fingered the smear of grazes and throbbing bruises at her cheeks, pulled the sleeve of her torn shirt to her shoulder, and spat out her words like a bad taste. 'Yuh had yuh fun with me, so what's stoppin' yuh?'

Larsen mouthed a curse, drew his Colt and swung the door open, the gun barrel already levelled on the space. 'Get in here,' he called as the first of the approaching shadow reached across the paddock like a cloud and halted. 'Shift!'

Esme shivered again, the sensation cold across her spine. Keep moving Billhook, she thought, her hands shaking, and you might stay lucky. Hesitate too long there and that finger on the trigger will sure as hell get itchy.

She swallowed, watched the shadow move on, grow and swing towards the open door. Hoofs scuffed, tack jangled, leather creaked. Her eyes closed as she imagined Billhook easing slowly from the saddle, hitching his mount, pausing, his iron-grip hands loose and flat at his sides. Vital seconds when he might just try Larsen's nerve too far.

'Esme?' she heard him croak. 'You all right there?'

'Cut the sentiment and get in here,' snapped Larsen.

Billhook's bulk and the gentle twitch of a smile at his lips, the concentration of his gaze on Esme, disregarding and dismissing Larsen as if he were no more than another item of furniture, seemed for a moment to empty the silence,

231

when suddenly, for Esme, the tick of the clock was real again.

'I figured for yuh mebbe needin' a hand here,' began Billhook. 'Doc said as how — '

'Shut it!' hissed Larsen, the drawn Colt tightening. 'We ain't here for folksy chattin'.' He kicked the door shut again. 'Who's out there? Doc and them sodbusters waitin' on me? What they send you for? Ain't got some fool notion of yuh lookin' to the woman there, have they?' He spat across the floorboards. 'Too late for that. She comes with me when this is done.'

Billhook's shoulders stiffened. 'You got any sense at all, mister, yuh'll pull out now. Step through that door and yuh dead. Yuh got my word on it.'

Larsen relaxed, the gun butt softer in his hand, stance looser, the washed eyes sinking to sightless slits. 'Well, now,' he drawled, 'I might just be tempted to show them skulkin' scum out there exactly what sorta business I'm about here. Half a mind to put yuh right back on that horse of yours — 'ceptin' this time yuh won't be seein' where you're goin'. Whole sight too dead for that! What yuh say, lady? We send this rat back to its hole?'

Esme had not moved, barely shifted a finger or stifled the tingling chill at her spine, and left the slow trickle of tears to drip from her chin. Would Larsen shoot if she made a dive for the door; could she reach for the bottle on the table, hurl it at Larsen's head, turn to the cabinet, fumble for the shape in the corner?

Would so much as the twitch of a muscle spark Larsen's Colt to a blaze that would blow Billhook apart?

But, damn it, just standing here, waiting — always waiting — when she should be doing something, anything . . .

The shattering crash of broken glass came behind the snorting roar of the single shot that seemed to rip deep into the foundations of the homestead.

Larsen pinned himself tight to the door as the splinters of glass flew like frosted flotsam across the living-room floor and the lead buried itself in the wall behind Esme. Billhook swung round, fists already clenched, and launched himself at Larsen, only to reel into a blinding daze at the lash of the barrel of the Colt across his temple. Esme staggered, eyes wide on the gaping gash of jagged pane and scorched windowframe, the sunlit space beyond, and shivered at the suddenness of the silence and the smoke of the shot that lingered on it like a breath.

'Stay right where yuh are, lady,' croaked Larsen, crouching low as he stepped clear of the prone sprawl of Billhook to cross to the far side of the room, the sweat gleaming on his face, eyes dark and probing. 'One wrong move and I start shootin'.'

Esme backed again, arms stiff at her side, and concentrated her gaze on the window space. There had been no mistaking the sound of the shot that had shattered it, the pounding, echoing roar, speed of the lead, the high, haunting whine as the blaze had begun its slow fade; a sound that lingered even now on the back of the silence, mirrored like a ghost in Larsen's face. He knew well enough who had fired the shot; knew that somewhere out there, in any one of a dozen shadows, the gunfighter was waiting and watching. And time was running out.

'Shift!' snarled Larsen again. He slid carefully to the door, lifted the latch, watched the bulk swing slowly on its creaking hinges until it stood fully open, and gestured with the Colt for Esme to move to the sunlit space. 'Get here, and don't figure on takin' one step further than I tell yuh.'

Esme swung her hair to her back, stiffened and came carefully round the table, shuffling clear of Billhook where he groaned and stirred in a pool of blood. Her stare settled straight ahead and steady on the sun glare and did not blink, not even when she was certain a shape had moved in one of the shadows.

She was still staring when the barrel of Larsen's Colt buried itself like a bone in her ribs.

22

'Yuh see what I got me here, fella? Yuh takin' this in? Yuh'd just better and come to some real careful reasonin' while you're at it, 'cus I ain't one spit fussed about puttin' some hot lead into this body. Not one bit, I ain't.' Larsen's gun barrel prodded deeper into Esme's ribs. 'Now you just get yourself outa them shadows you're huggin' and let's get this settled. Yuh got 'til ten, and I'm countin'. One . . . two . . . '

Esme flinched against another prod of the barrel, Larsen's breath hot and fetid on her cheek, her stare on the sprawl of shade from the wood store and barn tight and wet with a stinging sweat. Was there really someone there, would there be a movement, the sudden shape of the gunfighter stepping out to a showdown? She shivered. Would she be caught in the crossfire?

'Five . . . six . . . seven . . . '

Still no movement, no sounds save the rasp of Larsen's breathing, the creak at the shift of a boot. Only the prodding closeness of the barrel, the assured grip holding it steady and level.

Damn it, was the fellow ever going to move? Was he going to simply watch, waiting on a trigger finger easing into action?

'Eight . . . nine . . . '

The merest hesitation now in Larsen's voice, the countdown slowing, his concentration tensed on the shadows, probing every inch of them for the slightest flicker of a moving shape, glint of the sun on the Peacemaker's lift as it ranged to its target.

'Yuh clean out of time there, fella,' growled Larsen. 'Yuh ain't showin', so the lady goes. Your choice.'

Esme made to move, only to feel Larsen's free hand grab at her torn shirt, pulling her body tight to his side. Her stare blurred on a lathering of sweat, spinning the shadows and bulk of the buildings to a shapeless mass in the glare of the sunlight, her mind reeling on soundless images of Clyde, the faces of the neighbours, the floppy-hatted innocence of Sara Medley, the grey anguish of Widow Bishop, clinging desperately for a moment to the hope of a sight of Doc McLean.

And then the crash of a chair across the veranda and the looming, staggering shape of Billhook, his bulk filling the doorway like a chiselled slab of granite.

Larsen swung round, his Colt blazing into a shot that was already spitting high and wide of the blacksmith under Esme's twist and lunge. Billhook crashed on, arms flying, boots pounding thick and heavy to the boards, a growl growing in the pit of his stomach to a thundering roar that rolled from his throat like the anger of a storm.

There was another shot, another crack and hiss of splintering as lead bored into timber. Esme spun herself clear of Larsen's hold, fell back to the veranda steps and was scrambling in the hot dirt as the barrel of the Colt cleaved the air to thud across the back of Billhook's head and send him spinning against the wall of the home in a swirl of limbs and choking body.

That had been the moment when Esme should have scrambled to her feet and dashed for the shadows across the paddock, when the wood store and the barn had been only steps away from a darkness that would have swallowed her from sight. But she was too slow, too late in coming upright and was still on her knees when Larsen's grip settled again, dragging her back to the veranda, over the steps, to the threshold of the living-room before throwing her indoors to crash against the legs of the table.

Only then, as Larsen bundled himself into the room, slammed the door shut and settled his sweat-streaked face as close to the shattered window as he dared, did Esme squirm away, under the table, to drag herself to the cabinet.

Larsen was still watching, still blinking his haunted gaze on the shadowed paddock, when Esme found her feet, opened the cabinet door and fumbled silently for the shape in the corner.

★   ★   ★

'Hell, we should get down there and do somethin'. What we waitin' here for, anyhow?' Ship O'Toole stabbed the glowing butt of a cigar into the sand and squirmed against the bite of hot dirt across his shirt. 'Esme ain't goin' to last out much longer, and look at Billhook sprawled there. He ain't for a deal of action.' He spat sullenly. 'I'm for hittin' the place. What yuh say?'

'And Esme'd be dead before we got within shootin' distance,' grunted Henry Keyes.

'S'right,' murmured Joe Medley, squinting against the searing glare. 'What yuh reckon, Doc?'

Doc McLean tipped the brim of his hat to a tighter shading of his eyes and sighed. 'Devil and deep blue sea, ain't it? We make a move and Larsen'll sure as hell start flingin' lead like there was no tomorrow. We stay here and we're as good as condemnin' Esme to death.' He sighed again. 'Only hope we got is that gunfighter.'

'And he ain't exactly helpin', is he? Fired that one shot, took out a window and backed off. What's he figurin?' said Jonas Whitman, fingering the rough of his stubble.

'Seein' a sight more than we are, that's for sure,' croaked Doc, his gaze narrowing.

'So yuh sayin' we wait, that it?' said O'Toole. 'Damn it, I ain't for threatenin' a hair on Esme's head, but just waitin' and watchin' — '

'We ain't,' snapped Doc. 'We make a move, but we do it real slow, soft as shadows. We come up back of the home, blind side of where. Larsen'll he concentratin'. Get as close as we can,

242

and *then* we wait. See if that gunfighter stirs again.'

'Assumin' he ain't bleedin' to death,' groaned Frank Cooper.

Doc's gaze flicked anxiously to Frank's lathered face. 'Assumin' just that. Let's go!'

* * *

Esme stood with her back to the wall, her eyes aching in the gaze that followed Larsen's every movement, every flicker of nerve and muscle in his face and body, her fingers sticky on the handle of the short-bladed skinning knife gripped in her hands behind her.

There would be no second chance in this, she thought, her mind reeling at the prospect; no time to judge the moment, manoeuvre into position; no single instance when the gloom of the room might lift, the stifling air thin, or Larsen relax his guard. She would simply attack — just as soon as she could control the shivering and

243

summon what might very well be the last of her strength.

She took a deep breath, flexed her fingers on the handle, the smooth wood wet to her grip, and watched Larsen as he edged away from the window and reached the bulk of the closed door. His free hand lifted the latch, inched the door open a chink against the top of his boot, waited on the fading of the slow creak, and listened motionless, gaze flat and unblinking, as if expecting to hear a step, see a shape.

Now, thought Esme; could she make it across the room before Larsen turned, plunge the knife deep as it would go between his shoulder-blades, or would he still have the instinct to swing round and let the Colt blaze at the scuff of her first movement?

She had gathered the knife tighter in her grip when the hiss of Larsen's voice broke over the clinging silence.

'We try this one more time,' he mouthed, a half glance settling on her from the green eye. 'Sonofabitch didn't shoot before, so mebbe he's nursin' a soft spot for yuh, eh? Get here!'

Esme swallowed, fingers already fumbling the knife to the waistband of her skirt and folds of her shirt.

'Move, damn yuh!'

She eased forward on slow, careful steps, skirting the table, one hand brushing it for support, the other hovering loose and trembling at her side, all set to reach for the knife if the moment came, if she had the time.

Larsen reached for her, grabbed her arm and heaved her to his side, the Colt barrel stiff as a dead finger on the sweat in her neck.

'Gettin' to know the way of this, aren't yuh?' His words clamoured like the touch of hot weeds at her ear. ''Ceptin' this time I ain't lettin' go of yuh. Yuh stay real close, right, followin' my every step? And yuh put one foot wrong, I'll blow this neck of yours to shreds.'

Larsen's grip fastened tighter as he eased the door open and slid once again to the shadowed veranda.

No sign of Billhook sprawled against the wall, noted Esme, gulping on a gasp of breath, her eyes spinning for a sight of him beyond the smears of blood across the boards.

No sounds. No movements. The silence clung. The shadows lay breathless.

Larsen eased on to the veranda steps, paused, clamped his grip on Esme, ranged the Colt, eased again.

Into the hot sand now, the crunch of it beneath their boots like packed hornets fighting for space.

Where were they heading, wondered Esme; for the barn, the shaded lean-to far end of the corral? Was Larsen planning on riding out, showing his back while he had the edge of a hostage? Where would he head, and would he still be figuring on the value of a human shield once clear of the spread? Perhaps Doc, the neighbours, Clyde . . .

The first shot spat and whined from

the shadows to lift the dirt at Larsen's feet. The second blazed a yard beyond him. The third hit the dirt again, loosening Larsen's grip as Esme struggled to break the hold.

'Damn yuh eyes!' hissed Larsen, pushing her clear under the roar of his gun at a target of little more than drifting smoke from somewhere close to the wood store.

Esme lay face-down in the dirt, her sweat spreading in a dark stain. Larsen took two quick steps to his right, the Colt still levelled on the shadows. 'Don't think I won't end it for her right here,' he snarled, shuffling another step towards the corral. 'Yuh fire that piece of yours just one more time — '

But it was not the crack and whine of the gunfighter's lead that split the silence in the next seconds. Esme shuddered at the sudden grinding creak and groan of wheels, a tremor that gathered momentum across the sun-baked paddock, seeming then to roll somewhere deep beneath her as if a monster worm had stirred below the surface.

She raised her head a fraction to see the bulk of the homestead wagon trundling over the dirt, bearing down on Larsen where he stared suddenly wide-eyed and open-mouthed at a mound that rolled on of its own ghostly volition, unaware of the heaving sweat-sodden bulk of Billhook straining every muscle of his body bent to the wagon.

Larsen cursed, fired wildly into the timbers, dodged to one side as the shadow of the mass closed over him like a curtain, lost his footing and fell to one knee, his gaze riveted now on the wagon. He cursed again, but the sound was lost on the groan of wheels.

Esme struggled to her feet, reeling back, wheeling to left and right, away from the trundling mound, the ranging Colt in Larsen's frenzied grip.

Billhook had collapsed under a final, heaving push that had given the wagon its full momentum, blood and sweat clouding his gaze as he watched the bulk force Larsen into a skidding lunge towards the corral.

It was a long minute then of spinning wheels, screaming axles and creaking timbers before Esme had somehow stumbled back to the veranda, watched Billhook wince in the agony of the effort of scrambling for the cover of the open-sided barn, Larsen finally staggered to the corral fence, his lips slanted on a dirt-smeared snarl, eyes gleaming in crazed glances.

The wagon had come to a crashing halt against the far sprawl of the paddock fencing, the silence in its suddenly lifeless lean seeming to drench through the mist of dust clouds. Esme shivered, wondering if she might risk a dash to the barn to look to Billhook and had eased as softly as she could summon into the shadows of the veranda, when a shape, at first blurred and barely moving, grew in the depths of the wood store.

Larsen tensed, the grip on the Colt tightening, the frenzied glances settling to a cold, narrowed stare. He pushed himself clear of the fencing, stiffened taller and leaner in a firmer stance and spat deliberate carefully into the sand.

'So we finally get to it, eh, mister?' he called on a croaking voice. 'Got y'self an edge there, yuh reckon? Well, don't go figurin' too certain on it, fella. That woman there ain't goin' no place, 'ceptin' with me when this is done.' He spat again, glanced hurriedly over the spread. 'And if there's any more of them two-bit townfolk and sodbusters lurkin' out there,' he shouted, 'yuh take good note to stay right where yuh are. This'll be over real soon and me and Mrs Green wavin' our farewells. First to raise a hand against me covers it with the woman's blood. Yuh hear that? Yuh readin' me clear?'

'See yuh in hell first!' hissed Esme to herself, shifting again in the shadows, and then freezing in her shuffle as the shape in the wood store stirred again.

This time there was a boot, a leg, the dark outline of a body, the merest flicker of a brighter shape, something long and tight as a shaft of stray light. Esme saw only the softest blur of the gunfighter's face as he grew like a black hawk on the unrelenting glare, caught what she thought might have been a glance, the faintest movement of lips on words that had no sound, then blinked and felt the sweat run cold and icy in her spine as the man came on, the Peacemaker glinting in his grip.

She saw the blaze of Larsen's Colt, heard the roar shattering the silence, saw and heard his second shot, and still the gunfighter came on as if he were neither real nor there and the shots had passed clean through him.

She backed deeper into the shadows, expecting to see the gunfighter fall, soundless, almost shapeless, and bit into her lips as the Peacemaker came to life, the shots screaming, whining in an endless roar that rolled over the land until it seemed it had devoured sand, sun, dirt and sky in gluttonous, unremitting gulps.

There were faces surrounding her, hands at her shoulders, gripping her own, when she opened her eyes again. Voices tumbling in meaningless phrases, bodies gathering, closing protectively before she moved through slow, shaking steps to the body sprawled in a blood-soaked mess at the corral fence.

Larsen's empty gaze had no colour, she thought, staring into the twisted face. Now there was only a darkness, deepening to bottomless pits where light had no place and night its dead lair.

23

'And that, gentlemen, is that. End of the line. Ain't no point in goin' over it again.' Doc McLean mopped the sticky sweat from his brow, sighed wearily and leaned back in the saddle. 'We agreed?' he asked.

'I guess you're right,' grunted Joe Medley, scanning the sun-scorched shimmer of the Utepan. 'Can't say we didn't try, but it leaves a whole lot to fret on.'

'Say that again,' croaked Henry Keyes, running a hand over his neck. 'But yuh want my opinion on it, only two things could've happened: one, that fella rode out and somehow cleared the 'Pan, or, two, he got to endin' up much the same as we found him first time round, only we didn't get so lucky and find him again. I'd bet on him bein' crow meat, but God knows where.'

'Just don't seem right,' mouthed Frank Cooper sullenly, 'not when yuh figure what he did and how we've come out of the whole damned mess.'

'Well, some things ain't for dwellin' on,' murmured Doc. 'We got more than the gunfighter to be beholden to. We got Clyde here.'

Clyde Green smiled and rested his hands on the loose reins. 'We got what was ours by right,' he said quietly. 'Thanks ain't due. I got to Carver, stated our case, won the day, and we got the railroad runnin' through fifty miles short of our spreads. We're here. We're stayin'. We got a future.'

'Sure we have,' said Joe, 'and there ain't a body among us not offering up a prayer for that. Good men died in the cause of it, but what about the gunfighter? Hadn't been for him yuh wouldn't have made it to Carver, would yuh, and there just ain't no sayin' what Larsen might've got to given a free hand. So what did the gunfighter get — savin' some place to mebbe die like a mangy dog with nobody lookin' to him and mebbe not so much as a marker to show for it?'

The five men sat silent and thoughtful for a moment, their shadows long and black over the baked dirt, mounts flicking their ears against the drift of midday flies.

'Got what he came for, didn't he?'

Four waiting gazes turned to Doc, settled on his face, watched the slow, meandering lick of his lips.

'True enough,' he went on, his stare steady and tight on the far horizon. 'Never said as much — never said a deal, come to it — but I could read it sure enough. It was there. Somewhere, sometime way back; some grudge, a double deal . . . who can say in the lives of men who live by the gun? Larsen was his man; Larsen paid the final price, just as the fella always planned it. And what he found here, in Mission, out here among you farmin' folk, was just another example of Larsen's evil. Larsen paid for that too. Whatever future there is out here — buildin' up a decent town, farmin' good land to feed good folk — has been handed to us by the fella yuh brought in from the Utepan.'

'Bless the day we did that!' said Joe, slapping the neck of his mount.

'And tell yuh somethin' else,' added Doc, his stare narrowing on the empty sprawl, 'we wouldn't be doin' that fella one spit of a favour, by findin' him again.'

'Yuh reckon?' frowned Frank.

'What yuh say, Clyde?' said Doc. 'We leave it as it is?'

Clyde's gaze ranged the dirt and outcrops of the 'Pan, the scattered trail that petered into nowhere, the few gaunt shadows, stragglings of parched, broken brush, then swung back to the lands of the spreads, the curling spiral of smoke and the track that led to it.

'Womenfolk waitin' on us, I reckon,' he smiled softly. 'Darn near smell the apple pie from here! Let's get to it!'

There would be many nights like this, thought Esme, stirring to the gentle creak of the rocker on the moonlit veranda, nights when she would do no more than sit alone in the silence and gaze over the paddock, the outbuildings, the corral and the starry darkness beyond them.

But how often, she wondered, would her stare and her thoughts come back to the wood store, the shape of the man who had stepped from it; how often would she hear the roar and echo of the Peacemaker, see the twisted body of Larsen, dead in the hot dirt, the blood-splattered bulk of Billhook staggering to his feet?

How long before the sound of pounding hoofs, creasing leather, jangle of tack faded from memory and she was left with only the image, blurred and distant in the reeling ache of her head on that day, of the rider drifting towards the sun-blazed Utepan? Where had the gunfighter disappeared to? Why had he never spoken, said who he was, how he had come to be wounded, what assocation there had been between himself and Larsen?

Why, damn it, had he never said a word to her? Her of all people!

She eased the rocker to a halt and stared into the night. She was never going to know, and maybe had no right to answers. It was enough that the man had crossed their lives, been here, done what he did. Now there was only the long prospect of tomorrow, building the farm, watching the land prosper, the town come to new life. The future begin.

Even so, there would still be the nights when she would sit here, Clyde quiet and resting at her side, and remember, see the images, hear the sounds. And at some time in the years to come she would maybe get to telling the way of it all to whoever it was seated along of her.

Esme ran her hands gently over her

stomach, smiled softly and closed her eyes. She would give the good news of the baby to Clyde in the morning.

* * *

He might be dead before noon, or maybe later now that the trail had firmed up, the land mellowed to the long grass plains and a town taken shape way out there on the far horizon. Never any saying to it, was there, when a stranger rode in, tall and dark in the saddle, gaze watchful, hands easy on the reins? Maybe just a shade down on his luck there judging by the wear on his boots, stained pants and shirt that had seen better days. Just no knowing . . .

Handsome-looking Colt though.

Other titles in the
Linford Western Library:

STONE MOUNTAIN

Concho Bradley

The stage robbery had been accomplished by an old woman. Twine Fourch had never heard of a female being a highway robber before. He followed the trail all the way to a dilapidated log cabin up Stone Mountain. What happened after that no one could believe even after townsmen from Jefferson found the old log house and the skeletal dying old woman. But before the mystery could be solved there would be two unnecessary killings, a bizarre suicide and a lynching.

GUNS OF THE GAMBLER

M. Duggan

Destitute gambler Ben Crow arrives in Mallory keen to claim his inheritance, only to discover that rancher Edward Bacon has other ideas. Set up by Miss Dorothy, who had fooled him completely, Ben finds himself dangling on the end of a rope. Saved from death, Ben sets off in pursuit of Miss Dorothy, determined upon retribution. However, his quest for vengeance turns into a rescue mission when she is kidnapped by a crazy man-burning bandit.

SIDEWINDER

John Dyson

All Flynn wants is to be Marshal of Tucson, but he is framed by the territory's richest rancher, Frank Buchanan, and thrown into Yuma prison. Five years later Flynn comes out, intent on clearing his name and burning for vengeance. Fists thud, knives flash and bullets fly as he rides both sides of the law and participates in kidnapping and double-dealing. He is once again arrested for a murder of which he is innocent. Can he escape the noose a second time?

THE BLOODING OF JETHRO

Frank Fields

When Jethro Smith's family is murdered by outlaws, vengeance is the one thing on his mind. He meets the brother of one of the murderers, who attempts to exploit Jethro's grudge in the pursuit of his own vendetta. The local preacher, formerly a sheriff, teaches Jethro how to use a gun. With his new-found skills, Jethro and his somewhat unwelcome friend pit themselves against seemingly impossible odds. Whatever the outcome lead would surely fly.